Earth Cry

FOR LITERARY HEAT

www.barbarianspy.com

WARNING: This book is for sale to **ADULT AUDIENCES ONLY**. Contains graphic gay male sex, reluctance, multiple partners, anal sex, and gay love all of which may be considered offensive by some readers.

All sexually active characters in this work are at least 18 years of age.

BarbarianSpy
Jindalee St
Toronto, Australia

Earth Cry

by

habu

Table of Contents

Introduction

Man works both for and against the earth, and in these seven variously mystical, damning, challenging, and humorous Earth Day–themed stories, habu strips the relationship of human beings to the Earth and heavens—at or near the beginning of time—down to the basic elements of man's relation to nature and spirit in a primitive-beat, erotic mix of different approaches to shared fundamental questions. Who is in charge here? And how do we, as human beings, connect to and adjust our own basic wants and desires to the glories and delicate balance of the universe?

Starting back before time began, "Strip Evolution" is a tongue-in-cheek explanation of the creation story. Moving along in time, "Out of Sun" depicts primitive man seeing earth rhythms as messages from the gods that man had to serve and try to manipulate. The attempt by man to both serve and manipulate the earth in a primitive environment continues with "The Provider." "Hey, Good Buddy," moves the anthology into the modern world with a humorous ditty of two park rangers using environmental concerns to score with a young, unwitting fisherman. The humor continues with a misunderstanding in dealing with hazardous electronic waste in "Hijacked." Turning serious, both "Marsh Assault" and "For the Glory of the Earth" deal with the fight of environmentalists against those who would defile and degrade the Earth in their greed for short-term profit.

Strip Evolution

"Could you two p-u-l-eeez settle down? Look and see what you've made me do."

Gude snorted and Yeval giggled as they viewed the sphere hovering in front of Alnor, one ring circling its middle, but the second, larger one, askew, its spin causing the sphere to wobble. Alnor was rubbing an elbow that had been jostled as the two imps were chasing each other about.

"Sorry, Alnor," Gude murmured.

"I think you should leave it that way," Yeval cooed, a look of mock innocence on his face. "We haven't seen the effect of a wobbler, yet. It might be fun."

"This is serious work, not fun," Alnor said with an admonishing stare at Yeval. But then Alnor chuckled and said. "No matter. What was created can always be discarded and restarted anew. No big deal. But why don't the two of you stop thrashing about and do something quiet for a change?"

Gude and Yeval looked at Alnor expectantly, waiting, as always for Alnor to take care of them. The answer to any predicament was to expect Alnor to fix it.

Alnor was busy fiddling with the ring, gently moving it in one direction and then the other, with little effect, so it took a few eons to realize that four eyes were following every movement and waiting expectantly for guidance. Alnor sighed at the recalcitrance of the ring and then noticed, with a slight start, that the two gremlins were still there.

"Oh, I know. How about a game?" Alnor leaned over and dug down into a box of spheres of all sizes. Coming up with a smallish, blue-green one, Alnor held the sphere out to the two imps, who stood there, moving from one foot to the other, Yeval with a thumb in his mouth, and Gude already slitting his eyes and looking from pillar to post for an opportunity to upset an applecart or two. "Here take this. It's not choice enough to worry what you do with it. How about a calm little game of strip evolution? That should keep you out of my hair for a while—and you might create something interesting and useful. A round of coupling should settle you two down."

The two stood there, looking from the pitiful little sphere Alnor was holding forth and then back at the box full of nice, plump spheres. And then Gude smiled, grabbed the sphere and raced off—with Yeval in his tracks, the layers of his flowing mantel flopping around him.

Alnor sighed, grabbed the rim of the lopsided larger ring around the sphere hovering in space, gave it a good jerk, and then gave a little laugh as it clicked back into alignment with the first ring.

"Me first," Yeval demanded when the two of them were settled in a cloud of pillows with the small blue-green sphere hovering between them. "Give me the firop. I go first."

"Always you first," Gude started to complain. But then he shrugged his shoulders and smiled. "Well, OK, I don't mind."

Yeval cast the firop and then Gude did so as well.

"Sorry," Gude said.

"Crap," Yeval exclaimed. An efty right off the top. "Alnor must be looking over you for you to have such good luck."

"Shhh," Gude mouthed. "You know the rules. You have to remove something, and I get to choose, because I won that round. OK, off with your overmantel."

"Fine with me," Yeval said. "It's too hot up here anyway." But it wasn't hard to see that Yeval was sulking as he took off his overmantel. It wasn't that Yeval was opposed to shedding clothing; Yeval did not like to lose.

Meanwhile Gude was studying the sphere. "I get to do something with this too now." He studied it with deep concentration until Yeval started to complain that Gude was holding up the game. At long last, though, Gude sighed and muttered, "I know." He reached out and flicked the sphere, and it began to spin slowly. And then he raised his hands, snapped his fingers, and a light came on from across the chamber. The beam of light was directed at the sphere and lit up one side of it as it spun there.

"Foul," Yeval yelled. "That was two things."

Gude looked a bit bleary eyed. "I only meant to spin it; the light thing happened on its own."

"So you say," Yeval said. "I think you cheated."

"I'm sorry if you thought that," Gude answered in a crushed voice. "I wouldn't cheat. It just happened. Should we stop playing? I want to be fair."

Yeval sat there, pouting, for a moment and then got a sly look on his face. He knew what Gude was after and that, having started this game, Gude unlikely would let it finish short of a coupling completion. "Well, maybe if you take something off, it will be OK."

"And then you won't think I've cheated?" Gude asked. It was obvious that the thought of cheating really disturbed Gude.

"I'll overlook it this time," Yeval said. "If you take off your tunic."

Gude did so, and Yeval smiled. Gude looked very good with his tunic off. Very good indeed. Gude was the hirsute, muscular one. Yeval more willowy—and yielding.

Alnor had given each distinguishing aspects, but long ago Alnor had realized that the first two creation should also have been distinguished by separate gender. Alnor would not make *that* mistake again.

"And of course, I get to cast the firop again first," Yeval said.

Gude wasn't sure about this, but Yeval didn't wait. He picked up the firop and cast it.

"Hmm, pretty hard to beat," Gude said. But then he gave a cry of victory as he cast the firop and scrutinized the result. The mirth died in his throat, though, when he looked up and saw the angry stare Yeval was giving him. "An efty again. That does beat a double thisac, doesn't it?" he asked tentatively, willing it not to be so if that would wipe the scowl off Yeval's face.

Yeval was silent for a moment, but it was obvious that Gude *did* know that an efty beat a double thisac, so he just grunted and gave Gude a sour look. It wasn't that Yeval didn't like where this was heading; it was that Yeval didn't like to lose.

Gude didn't want to push the point, though, so all he asked Yeval to do was to remove his hair comb, which he did with a small smile, shaking his head as he did and making Gude catch his breath and feel warm inside at the sight of the luxurious raven-black curls cascading around his face.

Then Gude turned to the sphere and contemplated it. He placed his hands over the globe and waved them a bit, and the slowly spinning sphere responded to him. The colors were changing. The blue was getting bluer and a brownish-green was separating from the blue, until there were distinct areas of blue and then of the brownish-green.

Gude then gave a little laugh, being pleased by the effect he had made, and he looked back at where the light was coming from, his attention caught by the play of the alternating areas of light and shadow on the sphere.

While Gude wasn't looking at the sphere, Yeval leaned over with a scowl on his face and petulantly punched at both sides of the sphere with his small fists, causing lumps to rise on a couple of the brownish-green sections. He was going to hit it again, but he just managed to pull his fists back and replace his scowl with a beatific smile as Gude looked back at him.

With an apologetic look on his face, Gude picked up the firop and cast it again.

"Ah, that's a lot of nothing," he muttered as Yeval chortled.

Then Yeval grabbed up the firop and cast it with a fling of his wrists. "A thrice ewat. That beats you four ways from gesplot. Off with the breeches."

"The breeches? That's not how it's usually done. A sandal or something. This is supposed to be a progressive type of game. Slower, you know."

"The breeches. I get to pick." Yeval didn't even look at Gude as he shrugged and started to untie his sash. Gude's attention was taken by the sphere and what he could inflict on it. After a moment of contemplation, he leaned over and blew hard on it in separate puffs of breath. Areas of the blue retracted and sections of the brownish-green areas turned a dead brown color.

When Yeval looked back at Gude, he was pleased. Gude was well uncovered now, and had a hard body that made Yeval feel tingly inside and thinking all sorts of interesting thoughts.

Gude blushed and reached for the firop, but Yeval lashed out with his claws and took it up. "You forget. I won that round. So I cast first."

"Sorry," Gude said and pulled his hands back guiltily. The sorrow on his face was genuine. He had been disconcerted by the lusty look Yeval had given him—and particularly so, as he felt himself stirring inside. He knew where this was headed, but it was moving there faster than usual.

Paying no heed to Gude's distress, Yeval cast the firop hard and then hooted. "A virmic. I got a virmic. You needn't even cast. Nothing beats a virmic."

"Well, if I cast and got a virmic too—"

"Nope. Whoever casts one first overrides all. I win this round."

"I don't know. I'm not sure that's—"

"You're not thinking of cheating again, are you, Gude? Thinking that since I'm vessel and you're probe, you can just—?"

"Oh, no, no, sorry," Gude broke in, much in distress. "It's OK, you win. Don't cry. You win."

"Very well, then. You can lose that loincloth while I decide what to do with the sphere."

"The loincloth?" The words almost stuck in Gude's throat. "But . . . but, it's too soon to—"

"I get to decide. Those are the rules of the game. Of course, if you want to go all 'I'm probe, I know best' on me—"

"No, no," Gude said meekly. He reached down to his waist and started to unbind his loincloth. The look Yeval gave him—and what he was looking at—didn't help Gude as he stripped the loincloth off his pelvis. He tried to cover himself with his hands, but Yeval slapped them away. He could hear a deep rumbling down in Yeval's throat, which came out as a purr—and he felt his manhood rise.

"Please, the firop. It's your turn again," he said in a husky voice.

They both cast again, and Gude's upper chiam bested Yeval's inside rutki. Yeval gave no argument, feeling a little heated now and not at all averse to getting a bit cooler. As he unbuttoned and cast aside his middle mantel, Gude busily set plant life to grow on the unscorched parts of the brownish-green areas of the hovering sphere.

The next round went to Yeval, who punched the sphere with his finger, causing magma to rise up and create cones, while Gude was taking off a sandal—and while Gude wasn't looking, Yival slashed a great rift valley and a grand canyon with a swish of his fingernails for good measure.

Gude's single sefti was just too good for Yeval's nokye, even though it was a double—the presence of a britgo took away the advantage of the double—and Gude created separate heart-beating creatures for both the blue areas and brownish-green areas of the spheres after having snuck in an ordering of the seasons for the spheres.

Gude felt a little sheepish. This taking of two actions was clearly cheating, but he was beginning to feel his need and didn't think the game could go on very much longer—and he had just had a dilly of an idea what he wanted to do with the sphere. He felt he had to last at least one more winning round, or the sphere would not be perfectly balanced.

Still, Yeval was not playing fair either. While Gude populated the separate areas of the sphere with fishes and birds, Yeval was playing his hands over Gude's body and Yival was getting flushed and his breathing was becoming ragged—as, indeed, was Gude's.

Gude was quite sure that Yeval cheated in the next round—but in a strange way. Gude's cast of the firop had resulted in an inner ipoch, and Yeval's in a grand weatel. And Gude was quite sure that a grand weatel was the better throw. Yeval insisted, however, that his firop casting had gone out of bounds and insisted in casting again. Even the next case, a larow slam was better than Gude's ipoch, but Yeval tsk tsked yet again about something wrong with the throw that Gude couldn't understand and wasn't concentrating on, because now Yeval had a hand wrapped around Gude's phallus and Gude could think of little else. It was hard enough for him to maintain his focus on that last touch he wanted to make to the sphere.

15

On the third throw, Yeval cast an xotna, which was about the worst result you could get, and he cluck clucked his loss and started to move his hand on Gude's phallus in a most arousing way, as Gude did his best to concentrate on creating little reasoning beings in his and Yeval's images and setting them down on the brownish-green areas of the slowly spinning sphere.

Such was the distraction Yeval was creating, though, that Gude wasn't all that pleased with his handiwork. He thought he could do better—and decided that maybe later he would try to make the creatures a little less ugly and cloying. But then Yeval spoke, and he turned and drew in his breath.

"You won, and I know what you want me to remove," Yeval was cooing at him. His inner mantel was gone and he was arching his back to Gude and working the nubs of his boyish chest with the fingers of his free hand.

Gude groaned and lost all interest in what he had been doing with the sphere as Yeval pulled his lips down to the rouged nipples.

Still, while Gude was lost in sucking on Yeval's nubs, Yeval looked at the world they had created and he was displeased and angry. That last addition of Gude's had been a stroke of genius, and Yeval was jealous. While Gude fed on his nipples and Yival worked Gude's staff with one hand, he used the other to, first, guide his hands to the crease between Gude's buttocks, and then to reach out with that hand and flick the slowly spinning sphere with a system of recurring hurricanes, tsunamis, and earthquakes.

"There, let the little fuckers deal with those," he murmured.

"What, what was that you said?" Gude raised his head and asked as he tried to focus his glazed-over eyes on Yeval's face, not at all sure of the quality of the playful smile he found there.

"I said, the game's over, you win," Yeval answered, while murmuring to himself, "at least you think you did."

And drawing Gude's pelvis to him and guiding him into his passage with his hand, he whispered, "Let's fuck."

And so they did, suspended over the sphere they had evolved. They fucked for forty Earth days and forty Earth nights, and the sweat of their exertions and body fluids of their endless coupling rained down on and covered the Earth.

After they were done, they were both exhausted and floated off in separate directions to shower and refresh themselves.

Alnor glided into the chamber and stood, looking at the globe slowing spinning as it hovered midair, awash in the exhausted lovemaking of Gude and Yeval.

"Hmmm," Alnor murmured. "They certainly screwed this one up. I'll have to start all over again with it. And I've got to work out what I want to happen from my creatures coupling like that. There need to be some more complex differences than just surface looks."

Out of the Sun

I was happy that Ti had withered away within the last moon death, because there were now only eight elders in the village of the gatherers. But eight was more than enough. I was already bruised and sore as never before when Ai, the great chief, had taken his staff out of me that first time, having spilled the first of the seedings of the night before I was to die for the village. I did not care. Let the pain and the filling come, I thought. The danger for all of the people was near at hand. An offering to appease the mountain was needed. Once chosen, I did not care what happened to me on the night before the appeasement.

It was an honorable death. And death was ever present here on the more fertile side of the island, in the very lee of the thunder mountain. If scarce harvest did not take us, it was either the body weakening and sufferings, or it was the meat people from the other end of the island— constantly attacking us and taking, taking, taking. They were much larger and more robust than we were; we were like the sand before their crashing waves.

Ai was withdrawing and Ga had moved into his place. Ga looked almost sad. He had favored me for many moon dyings. I had found him enthralling and, as he favored me with extra food he had gathered and the murmurings of his longings and wishes, I had begun to mold to his desires. Now, as he gently turned me on my back and raised my hips with folded palm-leaf matting under my mounds, he whispered to me of his regret and sorrow. Regret that he had not taken me sooner, because if he had, that would have made me unfit to be selected for the appeasement offering. Sorrow that now this would be our only coupling, because on the morrow, I and the seeding of the strength of the village would go into the burning mouth of the thunder mountain.

Ga came in between my legs, and I arched back and cried out as he entered me. Ga was younger, more virile, and both thicker and longer of staff than the elderly, withering Ai, and for the first time my channel walls were being stretched to the limit and tested for their flexibility. I, also out of regret of what now would never be with Ga, held him inside me and stretched out the taking for as long as possible before his seed joined and mingled with that of Ai deep inside me. It was with a sigh and a groan that he gave up his essence inside me, and it was with a sob of loss that he withdrew his staff and turned from me, not being able to see what my eyes had to tell him.

The mean and vindictive Fre was next. He had wanted me when Ga was showing me favor, but there was nothing about him that I had found endurable. He wanted to own and turn everything to his pleasure, and he was not at all picky about what he would do to own it. Until Ga invited me to gather with him, once I had reached my season, I had to hide from Fre during the gathering. I had heard the stories of young men who did not elude him during the gatherings, most barely into their season, and how he had trapped and ruined them.

Now he was doing all he could to ruin me. I was bent over on my belly on the raised palm-leaf matting, and he was thrusting into me from the rear. Long, hard, rough thrustings. And he had fisted the hair on my head in one

19

hand and was cruelly arching my torso back to him. And he was slapping me on my sitter mounds hard as he rode me. The other elders were muttering and telling him to be more gentle, and I was pleading with him to slow and give me more time to take him. But he just laughed and continued on. He spilled his seed, but did not declare it, as ceremony required him to do. He wanted to enjoy me longer, so he kept on thrusting even as his staff was growing smaller inside me.

He could not fool the thunder mountain, though. The mountain knew he had seeded already, and the mountain showed its displeasure at his breach of ceremony. The ground underneath us began to move and groan, and the thunder mountain began to rumble its complaint that ceremony wasn't being followed. There were flashes of daylight outside the open doorway to the hut, as the mountain attempted to move the ceremony straight into the next sun birth—before all of the preparations had been made and all of the requirements meant. The wailing in the village at the verge of the beach conveyed the fear of the community of gatherers. They had been sad when I had been chosen, but this was our lot since the dawn of time. We merely served at the pleasure of the gods of the underworld, and we were privileged to live at their entrance at the top of the thunder mountain. It was a melancholy honor to be the sacrifice for my people. I could hardly bear to withstand their fear and wailing at thunder mountains display of its displeasure.

For me, this anger from the mountain meant the elders had to shorten my ordeal, and they clutched at Fre. Knowing of his guilt, knowing that he could not fool the thunder mountain as he fooled his fellow elders, Fre pulled away in fear, and the next of the elders quickly took his place and built up and spilled his seed as fast as he could.

The mountain quieted then, and the elders returned to a more decorous, leisurely fulfilling of their ceremonial duties—filling me with their seed throughout the night so that their authority and strength would go into the maw of the mountain with me and thus placate the gods of the underworld.

An hour before dawn, I was awakened, with an elder still crouched between my legs and mingling seed with seed as an offering to the gods. And I was guided, my knees almost unable to bear me out of the hut and toward the surf, now angry as well, coming hard upon the beach and crashing up in big fountains of spray. The sea felt the rumbling of the ground underneath our feet and joined in the angry demand that we atone—for what, we knew not. Had Fre done something else unspeakable before we became aware that the thunder mountain was demanding an offering to bring balance back into our world? I could only regret that Fre was not eligible to be sacrificed, although I was sure that the mountain would not accept him even if he had been untouched and pure before the ceremony began. I'm sure it would have just spit him back out.

I was dragged, more than guided, out to the beach, where the sand stopped and the sea grasses and the base of the palm trees started. There was a large crossing of two palm trees there that were bent together and lashed to form an X. There I was lashed as well, arms and legs spread wide, the meeting of the palms in the small of my back, open and naked to the sea.

My first duty was to try to calm the sea as I hung there open to it, awaiting the dawn of the sun cycle. If the sea calmed, I would be spared for another sun cycle to discern whether thunder mountain calmed as well. If it did, I would be free and we would be saved. If the sea didn't calm—and it never had before when a ceremony was required as long as any of the villagers still with memory could recollect—I would be carried to the top of thunder mountain and thrown into the burning maw of the mouth of the gods with the hope that this would be the gatherers' deliverance.

I hung there in what I knew were to be my last hours, welcoming the rebirth of the sun, hoping for it, as all of the villagers did as well. Sometimes, legend told us, the sun had not been reborn on the sun cycle of the thunder mountain celebration—the sky had remained as black as the sun death cycle. On these occasions, custom required that all of the unseasoned boy children in addition to the newly seasoned offering were to be given to the thunder mountain.

We had lost too many of our boy children this season cycle already—to a wasting away and to a raid from the meat eaters from the dark forest that separated our two peoples on the island. We could not lose more and survive as a people.

But as hoped for, at the moment expected, a glint of reddish-yellow light appeared across the horizon out into the sea, and a cheer of relief and joy went up from the gatherers assembled between where I was hung and the village. The sun was being reborn. And gloriously so. The reds and yellows and oranges and purples as the sliver became a line and then a widening band, were heartening to all. Only I would need to be given to the gods. And, as afflicted and sore and bruised as I was, I rejoiced with all of my people.

The sun rose from the water to greet us and to promise life and sustenance, and the people continued their rejoicing.

My rejoicing abated, however, and slowly dawned into a new fear, a new concern of imbalance and danger. I waited as long as I could, willing myself not to see what I was growing to know was a reality.

When I could contain myself no longer, I bellowed out a warning, sending my clarion call above the cheering and rejoicing of the gatherers. "Warrior canoes! The meat eaters! Coming out of the sun in abundance. Run, run for your lives."

It took several moments for the gatherers all to hear me, but no one here was too old not to know what the war canoes of the meat eaters boiling out of the sun in the morning meant.

Shortly I was alone, tied to the crossed palms. A lone offering now to the wrath of the meat eaters, as my people melted into the forest beyond the village.

What had we done so wrong as to bring this upon ourselves, I wondered, as I strained against my bonds, trying to break loose and escape. Thunder mountain was adding its displeasure; it had resumed its rumbling, and the ground was moving in waves again—and the waves were crashing more heavily on the beach, sending curtains of foam into the a sky that was darkening. The sun was dimming, perhaps having decided to leave us to our fate.

And then they appeared, as if ghosts, through the curtain of sea spray. Big, bulky men, heavy of muscle, tall of stature, larger and more robust than any of the gatherers. Naked, covered with fierce tattooing, and their staffs thick and long, swaying heavily between their legs as they strode out of the spray. Their eggs bigger than bird's eggs and hanging low. I moaned at the thought of the stories I'd heard of youths who had been captured by them and had escaped back to the gatherers—but not until after they had been sorely used and stretched and split by the meat-eater monsters.

They were all carrying clubs, ready to raid our stores after a good harvest. Striding in front was a particularly large and muscle-bulging warrior, painted for conquest, and obviously the leader of the raiding party.

He strode up close to me, blocking the light from the saving sun, as I writhed on the crossed palms, still trying to free myself. A nearly equally gigantic meat eater moved to stand beside him. The leader waved for the other raiders to continue on into the village, in search of grain and conquest.

The leader of the band laughed at my feeble attempt to escape. He backhanded me once across the mouth, which sent my head snapping to one side. And, as I was trying to bring my vision back into focus, he leaned down, and cut away the bonds at my ankles, grabbed the backs of my thighs in his big, strong hands, and lifted and spread my legs.

I screamed to the gods of thunder mountain for relief and release as he crouched under my raised hips and thrust his splitting staff up into my already beleaguered channel. All I wanted to do at that moment was to die, and the staff of the leader of the raiders was so long and thick and was being thrust so hard inside me that I thought I was soon to have my deliverance.

But the dark period of taking and the flooding of my insides with the seed fluid of the village elders gave me enough protection to stave off death, although it also denied me the relief of unconsciousness. I found that even when the other meat eater who had stopped before me with the band's leader moved to behind me, grabbed my hips with his big, calloused hands, and set his staff to working inside me in countermotion to his leader, I still could not drift away from this ordeal.

All I could think was that I would not reach the fiery mouth of the gods alive, and even if that were possible, I now was defiled, because the leader of the meat eaters was already jerking and grunting and flowing his accursed seed inside me. As he did so, his hand left my thigh and he grabbed up his club, and I knew my time had come.

But just as he was about to strike and the second man was pumping his seed deep inside me, the rumbling of the thunder mountain turned into true thunder, and the sky blackened. And then it was replaced by brilliant light. And from out of the sun, straight down from out of what was now revealed to be the risen sun, came balls of fire. Hitting the ground and hissing. Hitting the thatched roofs of the village huts and setting them afire. Setting the very palm leaves over our heads afire.

Pandemonium suddenly reigned among the raider band of the meat eaters, and they were running back out of the village, almost entirely empty-handed, and dashing for the canoes through the stormy surf. My assaulters were among the first to reach the canoes and to start paddling them hard back out to sea.

Almost as soon as the mountain's anger had started, it ceased. Totally. Although the balls of fire still hissed in the sand, they were quickly turning from bright red and yellow to a grayish black. The earth no longer was moving; the mountain no longer was rumbling. The sea had calmed. The raiders, however, could not see this. They were far down the island coast and out to sea now, racing back to their own people. Not looking back at what would now be seen as a formidable defense of the gatherers against raids.

It was all becoming quite clear to me now. The thunder mountain wasn't angry with the gatherers. The thunder mountain was pleased with us. So pleased that it wanted to protect us from the meat eaters. We were blessed.

As the villagers returned, tentatively, led by the eight elders, I was testifying in loud voice to how the mountain had saved us and prophesying that it would protect us from raids from the meat eaters as long as their warriors could speak of the events of this sun cycle.

Ai approached me, perplexed, and Fre immediately started nay saying me, saying that I was only trying to escape the ceremony. But Ga interceded, declaring in commanding, reasoned tones that all that I had said had come to pass had, indeed, come to pass. He challenged Fre to pick up and hold one of the mysterious, still-smoking stones that had appeared in profusion on our beach if he spoke the truth. Or to explain what limited amount they had all seen and heard while they were hiding in the forest. The sky had darkened. The sea had been angry when they ran away and was calm now. The mountain no longer was speaking to them in its anger; the earth was not trembling its ire beneath our feet.

Fre leaned down to take up a hissing stone, but as he drew near, a grimace set on his face and he snatched his hand up and turned and walked quickly into the now-smoldering village.

If I was lying, Ga went on, pulling the attention of all from the retreating Fre, what explained this calm that had fallen on them without the completion of the ceremony? No, Ga, proclaimed, the gods had accepted me as an offering as I was—a living offering. I had given the prophesy of long relief from the raiding meat eaters—who everyone here had seen with their own eyes—but who now had disappeared. I therefore was a true prophet of the gods of the underworld, fit to sit with the elders.

All were silent, and then Ga became bolder. He took the knife accorded to him by his position in the village and slowly, deliberately freed me from the tree. All the time he was speaking in commanding tones to all who were gathered about. He also, I must admit, being unsure of himself, kept one eye on thunder mountain to see if it would roar its displeasure at his actions. As the presumed elder who was to replace Ai when his time with the gods came, Ga said, he had much to learn from their new prophet. We would draw rations for three days and withdraw to the sacred ledge half way up to the mouth of thunder mountain, and he would commune with me.

Ga and I ultimately found the perfect position for communing, with him sitting on a moss-covered stone and me sitting in his lap, facing the great sea below and using the heels of my feet on the ground as leverage to rise and lower my now well-opened channel on his powerful staff as he stroked my staff with one hand and pinched my nipples with the long, elegant fingers of the other.

The Provider

"Where to do you go, Son of Waru? We are preparing for the hunt."

Tewaru walked on by his father, as if he didn't even realize the elder was standing there at the door of the hut. Waru knew that look about his son, knew that there was no reaching him when he was in one of his trances like this. It crushed the village chieftain's spirit to see his son, who in every respect was the natural ascendant to the chieftain position, in such a deranged state. He had tried to keep this behavior of his son from the rest, knowing that both Malru and Tadru were poised, just waiting for any sign of weakness from Waru and his clan that they could exploit to wrest power and make themselves the chieftain. Imagine what they would do if they learned that Waru's son was a shirker.

A shirker. That's what Waru had to admit to himself that Son of Waru was. Not just in the hunt and working in the fields, but where it was more important—on the mat in his hut, seeding the maidens provided for him and producing more sons for the clan. Tewaru was not doing it. And this was something Waru could not keep a secret for very long. Other families had been offering daughters, wanting to meld with Waru's clan, wanting the handsome son of Waru to quicken their daughters to bring strong and handsome men children into their folds.

Tewaru was well formed—the most handsome of the men in the village, and magnificently built. He had, as all could see, the mightiest phallus. It was on this that Waru had maintained his position even when Malru and Tadru had seen that he himself lagged in the hunt and no longer had the carrying power he once had. Tewaru, the promise of the village's future, the one with the phallus that all of the village women wanted to mount and to steal the seed of and bring new life into the village from. And yet, even though he had been given his own hut, as far as Waru knew, Tewaru had not sown any of the village women to procreation yet.

And he could not keep this secret for long. The women would talk. Because they had been doing everything they could to cajole Tewaru to lie with them. Even if, the gods forbear, Tewaru preferred to ride the phallus himself, he was not a dunce. He knew what his position and responsibilities were—what his own clan required for its very survival.

And yet, here, when he was called to the hunt, he was walking in the other direction instead—and not responding to the touch of the village women as he passed. Almost like he was in a trance.

And these trances of Tewaru's were yet another worry for the father. It was almost more frightful to Waru that Tewaru may prove to be a seer. They already had a seer in the village—a man not to be trifled with, a man who had come second to Waru in the choosing time when the old chieftain died and who would not be pleased at the thought of another seer in the village, and especially not one of Waru's clan.

Waru could only stand there and watch what had been the promise of his clan—their hedge on position and existence—walk through the village, all eyes turned to him—in admiration for his comeliness, his magnificent body, and

28

the swing of his low-hanging phallus, but also with the edge of a question, sensing there was something not quite right, a rising fear that the delicate balance of power and serenity in the village was in danger—the sneers on the faces of Malru, Tadru, and the seer a signal of struggles and strife to come.

This close to the beginning of time, when societies were only starting to organize and to learn to assert their control over their surroundings and, barely, to harvest enough of the bounty of the land to sustain expansion of their numbers, the balance was all important. But this was also the time for the discovery of ambition and the desire to control the lives of others.

Tewaru walked as if in a trance out of the village and along the beaten path to the stream cascading down the side of the mountain from above the village to sea, just beyond the verge of trees from where the village was moved the previous season to hide itself from marauders from the sea. With each season, the village of Waru was becoming more adept at sustaining itself and not just surviving, but prospering.

He walked until he heard the voice of the stream, calling to him, singing to him. The singing waters were calling to him so seductively and with such ringing tones that Tewaru could not understand why the other young men of the village did not hear it. But they did not; the song was only for him.

He stood in the pool below the falls and listened to the seductive singing of the cascading waters. He felt the drops of the water caressing his body, making love to him. And his phallus became a mighty club and his breathing became labored. He was moaning to the tune of the falling waters, which beckoned him to lie down in the pool. He did so, and the current of the stream rolled along his body and began to carry him down toward the sea. The stream deepened and he floated in yet another pool as he lay, face down, suspended in time without the need to breathe, in the water. Fishes rose to him and surrounded his body, and they made love to him. They thrashed about him, in increased urgency and abundance, until he was in the middle of a teaming mass of fish, sweeping over and around his body. Caressing his ramrod-hard phallus, suckling on the bulb of the phallus, and lapping at his sensitive balls. Making love to him, and urging him, in turn, to give them his seed—which, in time, he did, with a mighty cry of release, the milky treasure spreading inside the teeming swarm of fish.

Spent now, he rolled onto his back and let the current carry him down to the sea, where, from the foam of the surf, he rose and walked slowly back to the village.

Tewaru was exhausted when he reached the village and walked with measured steps to the entrance to his hut. Standing there were Waru and a beautiful young maiden, plump and ready and tremblingly willing for mounting.

With a tired wave of his hand, though, Tewaru just waved the maiden away.

"How can you not do this, Son of Waru?" the chieftain asked, his voice full of pain and on the edge of anger. "You have duties. You know what is expected and what will happen if you do not."

"I cannot, sire," Tewaru answered, his voice faltering as if he had no strength. "I have no seed to give."

"No seed to give?" Waru asked, incredulous. And then he smiled. "So, you have been mounting maidens in the pool? All is good then."

"I have given my seed at the stream, yes, father."

"And which of the maidens . . ."

"I know not," Tewaru answered. "I only know that I am drained. And that I must rest."

"I wish to . . ."

But then Waru's attention was called elsewhere, as the village's fisherman returned to the beaten gathering ground in the center of the village, all laughter and cries of joy and delight.

Waru turned to find them weighed down with strings of the largest fish Waru had ever seen.

From the group, out stepped Tadru, master of the fisherman, who announced with pride and gloating, "See, Waru, see what I and my sons have done? Cast your wondering eyes on fish the size and number of which we have never before seen in the village? We will feast tonight and there will be enough for the women to dry and feed us well until the next harvest of our field."

Waru viewed the celebrating—and what had caused it—with mixed emotions. It surely was a great boon for the village. But it also was a great boon for the clan of Tadru. He could only look on with a smile on his face and a hand gripping at his heart as Tadru called forth all of the villagers to the gathering ground.

"Come, come one and all," Tadru was trumpeting. "Come see what the clan of Tadru has done for the village."

Waru turned to appeal to his son to step up to his responsibilities and his potential before it was too late, but Tewaru had already withdrawn into his hut and was sinking from this world into one of his own in an exhausted sleep.

* * * *

"It is coming," Waru called out from the center of the gathering ground as he pointed to the sky. Massive gray clouds were scuttling across the sky from over the top of the mountain, from somewhere inland. Looking out to sea, Waru could see that the clouds had awakened the waters and they were screaming angrily and reaching out for the sands at the verge of the sea.

Waru knew these signs. It was one reason he had moved the village inland. But had he moved it in far enough? At this moment if seemed like he had not.

Villagers were scurrying around, gathering up treasures that the gods of the winds were already trying to take possession of. Waru almost commanded them to stop and look to saving themselves only, as the winds, perhaps to intercede for his people and to assuage the anger of the sea, were carrying everything toward the sea.

He was unsure of himself, but even in his fear and doubt he knew he could show no faltering now. He needed two men. He needed the seer and he needed his destiny, his son, beside him as assurance to the villagers that the clan of the Waru would stand by and guide them safely into the next life.

He called. The seer appeared at his side, but Tewaru, Son of Waru, was nowhere to be found.

The seer made a circle in the sand in the center of the gathering ground and began his incantations of calming the gods of the scuttling gray clouds, as Waru directed the collection of the villages most valuable possessions—the fishing implements of the Tadru clan and the farming and harvesting implements of the Malru clan—and commanded the movement of the villagers farther up on the mountain side.

"And where is Son of Waru, old man?" shouted the seer, momentarily leaving off his incantations to sneer his accusation. He could see as well as Waru could that Tewaru was not there.

"I have sent Son of Waru to the sands to plead on our behalf with the gods of the sea," Waru answered indignantly. It wasn't true and the seer knew it wasn't true, but the seer did not feel quite powerful enough at the moment to challenge Waru. If he was able to calm the gods of the clouds and winds, though, he knew he would gather power—maybe enough power to rise to the position that should have been his already.

"Take the villagers up onto the mountain, then, old man," he said. "I will stay here and intercede with the gods of the clouds and winds."

He watched until the last straggler was beyond the fringe of scrub on the path winding up the mountain—and then he sought out the sturdiest hut he could find and hid from the gods there under a matting of palm fronds.

Meanwhile, at the top of the mountain, Tewaru stood, tall and stretched out, as the gods of the winds and clouds had commanded him to do. He held his arms out in supplication, while the wind whipped around his body, taking and raising his phallus, filling it out, and making love to his body with its swirling drafts. The magnificent young man groaned and moaned at the seduction of the wind on his body, his legs and arms spread wide, and his hips undulating to the moaning of the wind currents. Until, with a great cry, he released his seed to the winds. At that very moment, the gray clouds veered off to the east of the land and were gone, taking with them the strong winds, as quickly as they had appeared over the mountain.

When Waru and the villagers returned to the village, the seer was standing, arms upraised, singing the praises of the success of his incantations, in the center of the circle in the gathering ground. He gave a triumphant stare at Waru as he entered the gathering ground and then both he and Waru turned and followed the entrance of Tewaru into the village from the mountain with their eyes—Waru in dismay and despair and the seer with the gaze of victory.

"I do believe the sands by the sea are not in that direction," the seer said in the sweetest tones he could call forth.

Waru did not answer. He turned and walked toward Tewaru, as the young man, body deflated, barely able to drag himself down the mountain, struggled toward his hut.

"Come, Son of Waru," the chieftain said. "There is much work to be done to put the village right again."

"I cannot, I am sorry, sire," Tewaru responded in a weak voice. "I am worn to the quick and can only sleep."

Tears sprang to Waru's eyes, and he turned to where neither his son or the seer could see his expression. He felt the power and balance slipping away from him. And he was in despair, as he knew that neither the seer nor Malru nor Tadru could protect the lives and prosperity of the villagers as he could.

＊＊＊＊

"At the morning's light, We will begin the harvest of the field," Malru, master of the planting, muttered to Waru by the fireside in the shadows of the gathering ground. "We will need all of the villagers there. It should take no more than two cycles of the sun, as I have reckoned from my survey of the field. Will you be there?"

"Yes, yes, I will be there. Of course I will be there."

"And that whelp of yours? The one who never does anything in the village. Tewaru. Will he be there too?"

"Yes, of course he will be there." Waru could not keep the hurt out of his voice.

"We shall see," Malru said. Then he laughed and rose and left the embattled chieftain alone with his misery.

After a moment, Waru too rose and, by a circuitous route so that no would take note, approached his son's hut. He wanted an assurance of his own that Tewaru would be at the harvest. It was vital that he was. The other elders and the seer were closing in on them like beasts of the forest. With each passing day, Waru was more and more worried about maintaining the peace and the balance in the village.

But Tewaru was not in his hut.

Instead, Tewaru was out in the field, stretched out on his belly. The vines of the field entwined his body, encasing him from head to toe. And the vines were moving, undulating over him, moving his body in a rhythmic rise and fall, as his phallus was buried deep in the ground. For hours, the vines of the field moved his body and the ground opened

34

to him to receive his seed. Again and again and again his body was teased and caressed to release its seed. And again and again Tewaru gave new life to the nourishing roots of the earth's bounty. As Tewaru moaned and groaned—and cried out in passion with each release.

The next day, the villagers turned out for the harvest. And when they reached the field, they exclaimed in awe and delight at what the clan of the Malru had produced from them. Never before had there been such an abundance of food. The village was surely blessed by the gods—and by the hard work and faithful husbandry of the land by the Malru clan.

They harvested for five cycles of the sun. And on each day, Malru approached Waru with a sly look and asked where his son was. And on each day, Waru said he had sent his son to the mountaintop to thank the gods of the field for their blessing.

But both Waru and Malru knew Waru was not telling the truth.

And now Malru and Tadru and the seer each believed that he had gathered the blessing of the gods and the power of the villager's respect and good will enough to challenge Waru for chieftain. Each was still immature enough in his understanding of ambition that he did not see the danger of the schemes and hopes of the other two wishful usurpers. They each had their eyes directly turned to Waru, however.

And at Waru's declaration on the fifth zenith of the sun that Tewaru was on top of the mountain, the three challengers, as one, stepped forward and called all of the villagers to return with them to the village and wait for Tewaru's return.

As they knew would be the case, though, what they found in the village was a totally exhausted and spent Tewaru lying in his hut and snoring his life away.

As their raft was being pushed into the surf of the sea, the former chieftain, Waru, and the disgraced—and still weak from exhaustion—Tewaru, Son of Waru, looked back at the sands of the beach and beheld the three usurpers already beginning their struggle of personal power.

What followed for the newly named village of Pacru, after the former master of the hunt—the wiliest elder of the village, let the three usurpers destroy each other before he himself took on the cloak of village chieftain—were years of leanness, years of such famine and torment that eventually the village dwindled to dust. The fish disappeared from the stream; killing winds screamed down on the village and angered the gods of the sea, which rose up and covered the village, repeatedly with crushing waves and killing foam; and the vines of the field withered and died—as, slowly but relentlessly, did the villagers themselves.

And no one in the villager knew why or how this disaster had fallen on them.

Miles away, however, on an island teeming with game and food-bearing plants and caressed with the cooling breeze from the sea, a father increasingly came to realize the worth and virility of the son he now reverently called The Provider.

Hey Good Buddy

The two had fought each other to exhaustion, each one trying to master the other, until finally they rolled away from each other in the bed of ferns. Joe was the first one to laugh.

"Yeah, but who woulda' known?" Al muttered. "You're such a cute little guy, and you've been eyeing me. I know you have."

"That's because you're such a big hunk—a real bear," Joe answered. "I can admire good muscle definition as well as the next guy." They were both laying on their backs, resting on their elbows, only in their unbuttoned green regulation shirts and their boots. The two were sprawled side by side under the low, protective branches of a tall fir tree. They were far enough off the trail leading up to Lower Mesa Falls that there was little chance of anyone stumbling on them—certainly not a park ranger. Joe and Al were the only two rangers in this section of Yellowstone Park.

"I think I had every reason to believe that this was the muscle you wanted to admire," Al, the big bear, said, as he fisted his still-hard cock with both hands—without overlap. Then he laughed too. Al always laughed at his own jokes. Sometimes others didn't—not just because they weren't as impressed with his jokes as he was, but also because of his intimidating size and the thick matting of black curly hair on his deeply tanned arms and spilling out of the neck of his shirt. He tried to keep the growth down on his chin, but his five-o'clock shadow had been building since 6:00 a.m.

"That's a very nice muscle, yes," Joe answered. "But as we both now know, we both like to be on the giving end of a 'hide the muscle' game, so this has all been very nice, but—" Joe reached for his gray trousers and started to rise from the ferns.

"Hey, wait. You aren't gonna leave me in this condition, are you?" Al was gesturing at his prodigious hard on.

"What do you propose?"

"Ever jacked off with another guy? Or better yet, done a 69?"

Joe had, and they both therefore managed to come, but it wasn't easy going, and they had to apply more personal attention to their personal equipment than the project probably was worth.

"Kinda tame, wasn't it?"

"Yeah, for you too?" Al answered. "But better than nothing."

"But not better than what's possible," Joe answered after a few minutes as they lay there wishing it had been better.

"Meaning?"

"Maybe a bit of hunting would be rewarded."

"Out here? If you haven't noticed, you and I haven't seen much of anyone but each other for a couple of days—and we've both seen how much good that does. We could just go back to the station and put on a couple of DVDs. I guess I don't need to hide mine now or pretend like I don't know you've got 'em too."

"No, I mean hunting like in for real tail. You know what's down just outside the park near Ashton, don't you?"

"Sage brush and scrub pines?"

"There's a dude ranch down there too."

"Several of them, I think. So?"

"So, one of them—one of the ones closest to the park boundaries—is a gay dude ranch. And those guys come up into the park. I've seen them fucking inside the park."

"I'm not that much into just lookin'."

"Neither am I. I've seen them doing other things too. Interested in a little bit of fishing?"

"Fishing?"

"Fishing for pleasure. Oh, hell, get up and button up and come with me. We'll do a little bit of hunting and fishing."

Al had nothing better to do, so he just grunted, rose up out of the crushed ferns, pulled on his briefs and trousers, adjusted his shirt, and headed out in the direction Joe had already taken.

"Hey, wait up for me. Where we going?"

"Henry's Fork," Joe growled over his shoulder. "Upper branch. You comin' or not?"

* * * *

The two stood there, behind bushes and trees, watching the young guy for quite some time before they made a move. Joe had assured Al that it would only be a matter of time before they could make a move.

"See that pile of beer cans there? He can't last too much longer."

The guy was young, one of those blonds with spiked hair—too blond to naturally be his, although he probably wasn't too far off blond, they discovered when he took his T-shirt off and was just in shorts. The hair on his body was a light, blondish down.

He was thin, what you'd call willowy, with a nice body that was only lightly muscled, but muscled enough to say he wasn't too girlish. His face was sort of girlish, though, more pretty and sultry than manly handsome. His eyes were sort of broodish and his lips sensual and thick. He obviously liked jewelry, because he had multiple piercings with silver rings in them: an eyebrow, an ear, his lip—and when he finally rose up from where he was sitting and stretched and turned half facing Joe and Al, they could see he had a ring in his navel too. His shorts hung low on his slim hips. The curls of pubic hair from his groin peeking out from below his waistband showed light auburn tones.

"There, told you he wasn't a natural blond," Joe whispered.

"Sortta close, though. Looks kinda sissy to me," Al answered with a little snort.

"Out here beggars and choosers and such," Joe whispered back. "Besides, chances are good we won't be stuck with a third top with nowhere to go. I think he's kinda cute. You don't seem to be put off yourself. You've been workin' your yang for several minutes now."

"I'm so keyed up now, I could probably fuck a deer. I got a yin to use my yang."

"Shhh," Joe admonished. "I think we're about to be in business."

The young guy had been sitting beside a stream where water was racing across rocks in the streambed. He had been sitting next to one of several deeper pools of water, lazily casting into the pool with a fishing line on a bamboo rod and frequently looking away from the pool and taking a swig of beer from the six-pack he'd brought. He looked like he was down to his last can. And he hadn't caught anything, even though the flash of light off of fish scales where the stream raced between the rocks promised that there were, indeed, fish to catch.

The young man stood and stretched. He pulled his pole back from the water and wedged the end of it between two rocks, leaving the line dangling in the water.

The shorts the guy was wearing were cut-off jeans, with practically no leg to them. A beam of sunlight caught his body as he grasped his fists behind his neck and stretched, working out the kinks, showing off his torso to the best effect. Al gave a little growl.

"Down, boy," Joe whispered. "You're going to get a piece of that."

"You sure?" Al answered. "He's going to get away."

"I don't think so. Wait for it. Just a couple of seconds more."

The young man was gingerly moving out into the stream, moving from one smooth-topped rock to another, being very careful because he was barefoot. His sandals were sitting by the side of the stream next to his T-shirt.

Reaching the middle of the stream, the young man turned toward where the water was rushing from.

Al moaned as the young man unbuttoned his fly, spread the sides of his skimpy denim shorts, and fished out his cock. Holding that in his hand, he arched his back and began to piss in a long, steady, golden arch—into the onrushing waters of the stream.

"Now," Joe growled. Not caring how much noise he was making, he strode out of the tree line and to the bank of the stream. Al stumbled out of the scrub too, in Joe's wake.

"Hey, good buddy. Watcha doin'?" Joe called out in a thunderous voice.

Startled, the young man nearly slipped off the rocks and into the stream. As fast as he could, he jammed his cock back into his shorts, but he left the fly unbuttoned, showing a cascade of curly light-brown hair in the gap.

"Fishing," he answered, although it sounded more like a croak. He could clearly see that he was facing two park rangers. He could also see that the big, scary, bear of the two had one of the biggest and thickest half-hard cocks he'd ever seen protruding out of this fly and being held in his fist. He'd sensed he hadn't mouthed the world "fishing" right and was

41

about to say it again, but he swallowed the word the second time in the realization that he didn't have any sort of license to be fishing in a national park. He'd just slipped away from the dude ranch and come up into the park, following the bank of Henry's Fork. He'd come to the ranch for the fucking, but he'd been more of a sensation there than he had figured. He was fucked out for the moment—or at least had thought he was.

"Sorry, I don't have a license," he sheepishly admitted, not being able to keep his eyes off Al's club of a cock, "But I haven't caught anything. Maybe we can—"

"Fishing's the least of your problems, young man. What were you doing out there in the middle of the stream?"

"Just relieving myself."

"Relieving yourself, you say? Where did you come from? Did you come into the park from that all-men's dude ranch down outside of Ashton?"

"Yes, sir. I'm sorry, but I—"

"How old are you, son?" Joe was doing what he could to put on his official face and tone. It was hard for him to do and not laugh, though, with Al standing beside him and pulling on his meat. The young man was mesmerized by Al's cock. His own staff had come out of the gap in his shorts again and was standing up from his brown bush.

"Twenty."

"Yeah, right."

"I've got ID. There in my wallet, under my T-shirt."

"It's OK, I'll believe you. We can check the ID down at the sheriff's office."

"No, please," the young man moaned. "I didn't catch any fish."

"It isn't about the fish, son," Joe said with a mock sternness in his voice. "It's about that there pissing in the stream. Do you know where that water goes that you just pissed in?"

"Down the mountainside?" the young man answered. He sounded like he wasn't sure. And he sounded like he didn't know where this was going. He was licking his lips and staring at Al's cock, though, which had gone full hard in Al's hand.

"Yeah, down the mountainside. Past that dude ranch you're stayin' in. That water you just polluted is going into the water you'd be drinking in about a half an hour if you were down at that ranch. We take environmental protection very seriously in our national parks. We're gonna have to take you down to the sheriff's office in Ashton."

The young man moaned.

"Unless . . ." Al said.

"Unless what?" the young man whimpered.

"Unless you give it up for Ranger Al here and me. You come from that dude ranch, and I can see that you want it from Al. Open your legs for us both and we'll just overlook that pollution charge—even though we take environmental protection real seriously in this park."

* * * *

Joe and Al stood side by side, arms entwined, on the stream bank as the young man knelt before them and alternately gave each of their cocks attention with his mouth. They groaned almost in unison as he tried to take both cocks together in his mouth at once. Al was particularly pleased when he found that the young man had a ball stud in his tongue too—and knew full well what to do with it.

"Hey, lookee here. He's got a ring down here too," Al rang out with glee. The young man was stretched out on his side along a log, with Joe standing behind him, lifting his leg with one hand, and fucking him in a side split. The young man's head was arched over the end of the log and Joe was slow-pumping his throat with his cock. Al had just reached over to pay attention to the young man's cock and found the ring at the base of his penis, where the perineum began, and pulled gently on it.

"Look, it makes the cock bounce," he said.

The young man moaned.

Joe had claimed firsties, because it was his idea and his setup. Al good-naturedly acquiesced, with the comment, "You'd best go first. After I'd reamed him, he probably couldn't even feel you fuckin' him."

The young man came with Al stroking in his mouth and moaned and gagged as Al rubbed his tonsils with the bulb of his cock.

For Al's turn, Al was sitting on the log, and the young man was sitting in his lap, facing him, and fucking himself on Al's staff by leveraging off the soft earth of the stream side with the balls of his feet. He was crouching more than sitting, though, so that he only had to take half of Al inside him. Joe was standing behind the young man, with his hands covering and worrying the young man's nipples. He was nuzzling the young man's neck with his face and trying to tease the young man to turn his face for a kiss. But the young man was more interested in exploring Al's hairy chest with his hands and lips.

"Enough of this shit," Al declared. He grabbed the young man by his waist, lifted his body and then jammed it down on his cock. The slight blond howled as Al started pumping his ass on his cock, slamming him up and down, burying the monster cock to the quick with each pull.

The young man's torso flopped back toward the ground, and Joe stifled his cries by pushing his cock between the young man's lips and beginning a slow pump.

Afterward the young man lay on his back between the log and the edge of the stream, his arm flung over his face, and moaned quietly.

Joe and Al sat next to each other on the log, both looking satiated and very satisfied with themselves.

"Hey, lookee there," Al sang out, "I think you've got a bite. Better pull in your line."

The young man moaned. He didn't move.

Joe went over and pulled in the line. "Yep. You got one. And it's a beauty. For another fuck, we'll let you take it home, no worries about a license. And no worry about pollution, either. It came from upstream. Your piss is down at the dude ranch now."

The young man moaned. Al leaned over and grabbed him by the waist.

The young man went home with his fish.

* * * *

"Hey, we're close to the stream," Joe said, as the two trudged along in the park the next day. "We might as well check it out."

They didn't bother to approach the spot of the previous day quietly. They just tromped in, laughing and joking with each other. They surely could be heard from a good distance.

As they entered the clearing, Joe and Al stopped in their tracks, both taking on big smiles.

"Hey, good buddies. Watcha doin'?" Joe sang out.

Their young man had brought a friend. The two twinks, each wearing just skimpy denim shorts, with their flies unbuttoned, turned from where they were standing in the middle of Henry's Fork stream, both still pissing in wide arcs into the center of the racing stream, both having broken into broad grins.

The eyes of both of them went to Al's fly, where he already had his monster cock out, ready to give them both a lesson in environmental protection—which Yellowstone Park takes very seriously.

Hijacked

"What's good for the earth and all that."

"I often wondered how that worked," the young man behind the counter of the diner just south of Santa Fe said. He was leaning over the counter, having delivered Andy's breakfast, but not all that anxious to move on. Andy was a real looker. A regular young Paul Newman, but with more muscle. And the young man behind the counter had his interests. Besides, the looks he was getting back indicated that the trucker, Andy, had similar interests.

"Yeah, gotta do what we can to keep the environment clean," Andy said. He had been trained well to parrot his company's policies, but he did, in fact, support keeping the environment as clean as possible.

Sadie, the older woman behind the counter, snorted in passing, "Ya mean getting the environment *back* to clean don't ya, sweetie? Make up for decades of screwing it up." She nudged the man behind the counter. "There's an order needing taken at the end of the counter, Stan, if you can get your eyeballs back into your head." As Stan reddened and scurried off, she turned to Andy. "Top off that coffee, sweetie?" She didn't have any objection to hunks herself.

"Yeah, thanks," Andy said, as the man behind the counter moved to the far end of the barstools. There was a young guy, some sort of mixed breed perched on a stool down the counter. Some part white in him, Andy thought, but something else. Native American? Hispanic? Whatever it was, it was a good mix. He was kind of small, but well formed and with a real good face. Andy wouldn't mind getting his dick into that one, if he was legal. And the glance the young guy gave him after he'd given his order to the counter man indicated interest too.

Andy smiled a bland smile back. He didn't have to be the one on the make. He had no trouble picking guys up on the road to fuck silly in the compartment behind his cab. He knew he looked like a movie star and was hung.

While eyeballing the honey at the end of the counter—well both of them; the mixed breed perched on the stool and the guy behind the counter, although, of the two the mixed breed was the winner—and being eyeballed in return, it hit Andy that something seemed a bit strange. Then he figured out what it was. When he'd seen the mixed breed walking across the windows outside before entering the diner, he'd been chatting with three other guys. Where were they? Andy looked around the diner and saw that the three were over at a table. A surly lot, he thought. He must have been mistaken about the really sweet-looking mixed breed having been with them. They looked like ranch hands just off a cattle drive, and looking for trouble.

Sadie had made a pass at serving them coffee but had backed out of their aura as fast as she could. She was at the end of the counter now, pouring for the small mixed breed. They exchanged a few words and then she turned and called down the counter to Andy.

"You driving that fancy rig out there? Guy here asked about it, but I was curious too."

"Yeah, that's mine," Andy said. His semitrailer was parked across the parking lot, all gleaming silver.

"Guy here says he ain't seen nothing that fancy around here before. Neither have I. He said that's got to

47

have the biggest compartment behind the cab he's ever seen."

"Yep, it's a special model," Andy answered. "My home away from home. And the truck's a new-fangled design. Anderson's producing a few hybrid semi trucks now to see how they go. My company's motto is 'Anything for the Environment,' so I'm helping to test a hybrid model to see how it copes with hard hauls like the one from Santa Fe to Phoenix. So far so good. Good mileage for a semi, fewer emissions, and it's pullin' OK so far."

"What'yer hauling this trip?" the counter man asked.

"Electronic gear. TVs and computer monitors mostly. Taking them from Santa Fe to Phoenix."

Sadie snorted, "So much for the environment. Fancy earth-friendly truck haulin' ozone killers."

Andy was about to respond to that, when there was a growl from across the room. The three dusty cowboys wanted to order. Sadie pulled a pencil out of her hair and a notebook out of her pocket and sauntered off across the room.

Andy finished his coffee, tossed his money down on the counter, and went to the head to take a piss before going back on the road. He was standing at the urinal, pissing a strong arc onto the porcelain wall when he heard the bathroom door open. He turned his head a bit as the good-looking mixed breed entered and sidled up to the urinal beside him. The young guy unzipped and turned and gave Andy a grin. He then lowered his eyes to Andy's urinal. Andy turned a bit to give the dude a good look at his package. He was proud of it—and had every right to be proud of it.

The other guy gave a little gasp, and Andy had to move a bit to his right, afraid that the mixed breed would piss on his pant leg in his loss of control at seeing how Andy was hanging.

The mixed breed put his hand on the edge of his urinal—the side toward where Andy was standing. This was a known first stop in reaching down and touching the other guy's dick.

The truck driver might have said something, told the mixed breed to go ahead and feel his dick, as the come on seemed pretty obvious and the little guy was a really nice piece—and was equipped pretty well too. He was half hard just from looking at what Andy was packing, and Andy was about to give him an even better look—a feel even—when the bathroom door opened again and the man behind the counter entered.

The idea of a threesome—all the signals had been there—raced through Andy's mind. But he didn't really have time for this, and he was a bit worried what that Sadie would say when the three had been in the head for some time. She had a mouth on her and didn't seem to put much restraint on what she'd say at full volume. And she seemed smart enough to have caught the vibes going on between the men out at the counter. She certainly seemed to have had the number of the guy behind the counter. Andy just didn't want to endure the walk from the head to the diner door—and there was always something he could pick up on the road. He'd never had trouble that way.

So, he zipped himself up, having emptied his bladder essentially before the mixed breed had entered the room, and relinquished the urinal to the counter guy. There were only two urinals. If Andy didn't back out fast, there obviously was going to be some action or some embarrassment at misreading signals. The counter guy seemed much more interested in what Andy and the mixed breed were doing than in taking a leak.

Andy marched quickly through the diner and out to his fancy environmentally correct semitrailer. He had to walk around an old Mustang convertible with a faded red paint job and an even older beat-up truck that had once been a U-Haul van but had been indifferently painted over in white to get to his rig. He checked around the semi for anything that looked like it might be trouble. Finding nothing worrisome, he pulled himself up into the truck cab and drove out onto Interstate 25 for the short leg to Albuquerque through the Santo Domingo and San Felipe Indian reservations. He'd been a while checking the truck and the Mustang and van were still parked by the diner when he drove out.

His mind went to the bathroom he had hastily left and to what maybe the counter man and the cute little mixed breed were still doing in there. He sighed with a bit of regret, almost sorry that he hadn't stayed for some action. It was true he could pick a guy up between here and Albuquerque, but chances were good he wouldn't be as nice a piece as that little mixed breed.

He wasn't driving through the desolate sage brush area and alongside a steep ridge for long before he noticed that a convertible was riding his tail. The tailgater looked like a faded-red Mustang. The little piece from the diner maybe? And sure enough, not long after he noticed it, the Mustang pulled out beside him, coughing smoke out of its ass that made Andy frown. He couldn't keep the frown on very long, though.

The cute mixed breed was driving and was alone in the car. Andy looked down into the open-topped convertible from his high perch in the cab and did a double take and a little swerve of the semi in his lane followed by a big grin. The little guy had his cock out of his shorts as he drove and was beating himself off. He grinned up at Andy and then let the semi surge ahead and pulled in behind it again.

Now, if that wasn't an invitation, Andy didn't know what was. He'd see how interested the little guy really was.

In Albuquerque, with the Mustang still hot on his tail, Andy turned west on Interstate 40, headed for his destination in Phoenix. He knew though that he was taking a break soon, because the Mustang turned onto 40 with him.

Hot on my tail; tail hot for me, Andy thought. And he laughed at his joke. He had to spread his legs a bit because he'd gone very hard and his basket needed added room. He put a hand on his basket and rubbed. He was more than ready for some tail. He'd get a taste of the mixed breed after all.

He turned into the first rest stop he came to and parked far back in the truck lot. The Mustang didn't follow him into the truck parking, but he'd done this a hundred times before—hook up with a guy on the road and both pull off in a rest area to rock around in the compartment behind Andy's cab. Not usually this blatantly, but he was all the harder for it the way the cute little trick was playing it. He leaned on his steering wheel and looked out of the driver's window until he saw the mixed breed appear and start walking toward the truck across the expanse of asphalt. A real sexy walk. Oh, yes, he wanted it.

If he could go any harder, Andy would. What a sweet lookin' piece, he thought, as he climbed down from the driver's cab and opened the door to the spacious compartment behind the cab.

"Want to see the inside of my cab and do a little rockin' and rollin'?"

"Sounds good," the mixed breed answered, with a smile.

"A little suckin' and ballin?" No reason not to be direct, Andy thought. The little piece wasn't being shy.

"Sounds great."

"Just to be clear, you're doin' the suckin' and I'm doin' the ballin."

"Exactly what I had in mind."

The young man, who sometime during the process identified himself as Hector, which Andy didn't believe as he identified himself as Sam, pulled himself up into the aft compartment right behind Andy. Andy had no more time than to sit on the narrow bed in the rear of the compartment than Hector was kneeling between his knees, unzipping his pants, pulling out his hard cock, and starting to give him head. Andy leaned over and pulled the compartment door shut and then started searching around in a pouch on the side wall. Anticipating him, though, Hector pulled a condom packet out of his pocket and handed it up to Andy without losing a stroke of his mouth on Andy's cock.

After several minutes of what was a really excellent blow job, Andy tore open the packet. Hector reached up and clasped Andy's hand in his and came away with the disk. He lifted his head off the cock, popped the condom disk in his mouth, and then smiled up into Andy's face before lowering his mouth again and managing to roll the condom onto Andy's cock with his teeth and tongue.

Andy shuddered and gave a growl from deep in his throat. This was going to be good. The little piece really knew what he was doing.

Andy rose up, grasping the small mixed breed by the waist and turned him to where Hector's back was on the bed. Andy grabbed the hem of the young man's T-shirt on either side, Hector's torso briefly rose up off the bed as Andy pulled the shirt over his head. Then he stripped Hector's shorts off and unbuckled his own pants and let them and his briefs slip down to the floor of the compartment.

"You're huge, and gittin' bigger," Hector said. It came out in sort of a gaspy squeal though.

"You saw it at the diner and came for it. You think you can take it all?" Andy growled.

"Or die trying," Hector responded. He laughed and spread and raised his legs, finding footholds on the walls of the compartment. He grabbed for the back of Andy's head with both hands and guided Andy's face down to his. They hungrily went into a deep lingering kiss. Andy's hard cock was poking at Hector's flat belly, and the young man reached down with a hand and encased the dick and beat it against his belly as they kissed.

Breaking out of the kiss, Hector growled. "Don't make me wait. Fuck me, fuck me hard."

Andy wasn't ready yet, though, and he assumed Hector wasn't ready for the thickness of him either, so he slowly worked his mouth down the perfectly formed berry-brown torso, down to where he could swallow Hector's cock, while the young man arched his back, cupped the back of Andy's head. Andy already was working his fingers into Hector's hole, which was opening up to him nicely.

"Oh shit, oh fuck. Fuck me, fuck me," Hector whined as he ran his fingers into Andy's hair, pulling his head as closely into his groin as he could. "Now, now. Shit! Do it now!" he cried out.

With a laugh, Andy pulled his head out of Hector's lap, raised his body over the young mixed breed's, slowly forced his cock inside the channel as Hector writhed and moaned. Hector ran his hands inside Andy's unbuttoned shirt and up his hard-muscled torso, to grasp the truck driver's bulging pecs and then to travel on to dig his fingernails in Andy's shoulders, as Andy did it "now" . . . did it hard . . . did it deep . . . did it with increasingly possessive vigor.

With a cry, Hector shot up Andy's belly. But before Andy could come, the young man was scrambling out from underneath the older man and was turning them both on the narrow bed so that Andy was on his back and Hector was crouched over him. Hector sank his mouth over the sheathed cock, scraped his teeth back up the sides, and repeated the action again and then again and again. Andy arched his back off the bed and growled, ready to come, but Hector didn't let him come. He held the older man immobile for nearly a moment, while Andy came off his high.

Then Hector began working his mouth up from the cock, nibbling and licking at Andy's beefy torso. The younger man grasped Andy's biceps and pushed his arms over his head. Hector held Andy's arms over his head while he worked on Andy's nipples and Andy groaned and grunted. Andy shuddered and jerked once as he felt Hector straddle him and begin a long descent of his channel on Andy's cock again. Down Hector's hips came, as Andy moaned at the warmth of the channel and the undulation of the sweet little piece's channel muscles on his cock. Up and down. Andy gasped. This was one talented, tight channel. Up and down, and Andy gasped again.

Hector rocked back and forth and sideways on the cock and Andy raised his torso in ecstasy and embraced the young man tightly with his arms. They rocked back and forth, moving Andy's cock inside the tightened channel, Andy's moans a bass, Hector's a baritone. Once more Andy's body went rigid, ready to blow, and Hector held him in suspense of movement until the urge had passed. Then Hector gently pushed Andy on his back again and restarted a slow ride of the cock.

Hector's hands were gliding up Andy's arms, pushing them above his head, as Hector's tongue slurped into one of Andy's pits. Andy could feel that there was something in one of Hector's hands, but he didn't know what it was until the handcuffs had been snapped on one wrist, pulled through a metal handle bar in the side wall of the compartment, and then snapped on the other wrist.

"What the shit?" the trucker muttered.

"Go with it," Hector said with a low-throated laugh. "I'm going to give you the screwing of your life."

Andy shuddered. The little fucker already was giving him the fuck of his life.

The mixed breed swung around and pounded on the closed door and then he swung back toward Andy and began to fuck himself in earnest on Andy's cock. Andy groaned and grunted and arched his back in pleasure as the young man rose and fell on the cock and broke off from the rhythm to revolve his hips and to churn forward and back and from side to side on the cock. His channel muscles were working the cock for all they were worth. Andy groaned each time Hector took it all and then held, squeezing his channel walls on the throbbing cock. Andy noisily took in his breath as Hector slowly pulled up the cock and then gasped and grunted and his pelvis jerked as Hector slammed himself all the way down again. Again and again and faster and faster.

Andy gasped and muttered his, "Yes, yes, like that, there," mile-high pleasure. The sweet little piece was good . . . really good . . . the best. Andy had never picked anything this good off the road before.

Andy heard the rasp of the hinges on the rear door of the semitrailer, and he turned his head in slight concern. But Hector lowered his lips onto Andy's and they went into another deep kiss. Andy didn't care under the circumstances what was happening at the back of the truck. Who the fuck cared about that junk? Sadie in the diner had been right—it was all just a scourge on the earth. All he cared about was that he was building to an explosion. And Hector had to let him have it this time.

He heard the rummaging in the back of the truck. But he didn't care. He was in paradise and on his way to new levels of heaven.

The explosion of his ejaculation was matched with a pounding on the compartment door, which was jerked open. An angry raspy voice yelled, "It's a bust, Pete. We gotta beat it. Get out of there."

Hector was pulling himself off of Andy, while, still exhausted from the thunderous ejaculation the young man had given him, Andy wearily raised his head and managed only a, "What the fuck?"

"You were great. Wish we could do it again," Hector, perched at the opening to the compartment, said. He was grinning as he pulled his shorts and T-shirt back on.

"Wait. You can't leave me like—"

"Here's the key to the cuffs. You can keep them," Hector said, as he flipped the key onto the floor of the compartment, well out of Andy's reach, and, with a grin, was gone. As Pete, as Andy now knew the young mixed breed to be named, dropped out of sight, Andy got the blur of a van truck speeding across the opening. It was an old U-Haul truck with an indifferent slapping of white paint over it.

Andy lay there for an eternity, his feelings mixed. He knew he'd been hijacked and that Hector's ardor had all been to serve that. But, god, what a beautiful brown body. And man could he fuck.

A shadow fell over the open door to the compartment, and the body of a beefy young man filled the space.

"Lookin' might fine like that, Andy," the young man said. He was wearing a big grin. "Always dreamed to find you this way. Would have preferred that it be after you'd fucked *me*, though."

"What the fuck are you doin' here, Kurt?"

"What a way to talk to your savior—especially seein' as how you are all trussed up like this—completely at my mercy."

"What the shit happened? What'yer doin' here?"

"I'm driving a load of junk electronics to Phoenix for the company today too. Pulled into the rest stop and saw your semi with all that electronic crap out on the ground. Decided I'd check you out. Glad I did. You check out real nice."

"I was hijacked," Andy said.

"Yep, I can see that. Used a real nice diversion, I see. In fact, it reminds me of old times. While I'm ridin' that cock of yours, I'll be thinkin' that, if I'd used cuffs like that, I wouldn't have let you get away. I guess those hijackers were expectin' something else back there other than broken and used TVs and monitors goin' to them special incinerators in Phoenix."

"They fingered me in a diner south of Santa Fe. If they'd come in a little sooner, they'd have heard me telling the waiter that this was an environmental waste trip, not a load of new electronics. Now pick up that key down there and undo me."

"Think I'll just do you first, seein' as how you can't just slip away from me this time," Kurt said. He pulled the door to the compartment closed, reached into his pocket and pulled out a condom packet, and rolled the spent one off Andy's cock. "Whooie, what a load of cum you gave for him," he said as he dropped the used condom on the floor. "Hope you saved some for me."

Marsh Assault

The pain was fighting with the pleasure; the fear with the exhilaration. The struggle for the dominant sensation was sending my adrenaline through the roof. God, I was skipping along the top of the clouds. Shit, I was skimming the searing flames of hell. Pain, pleasure. Pleasure, pain. Right there on the edge. Would he love me or kill me? Would he fulfill my desires? Or would he take me to the edge of release only to abandon me to want and frustration? Either way, this was the edge that made me feel alive. This . . . this . . . this, right here, right now.

He had looped his belt around my neck and was arching my torso up toward his chest as he covered me at the end of my bed. The pressure was choking me. I don't know if this was better or worse—more painful or more arousing—than when he'd been grabbing me by my hair and jerking me back to him. He had the arm I wasn't stiff arming into the bedspread for some form of support painfully forced up my back with a strong fireman's grip on my wrist.

He was inside me, big and thick and deep, pounding my ass interminably, cruelly, gloriously. Would he never come? big, virile, young stud. Pounding, pounding, pounding. Fast and furious. I was gagging, whimpering, moaning.

My arm gave out and I collapsed on the bed, clutching at the choking collar created from the loop in the belt, almost blacking out at the tightening of the noose from the combination of him trying to jerk my head back and the weight of my body falling forward. He rode me down onto the bed, my belly on the edge of the foot of the bed, my knees struggling to find purchase on the carpet.

"Gonna come," he muttered. He released both the pressure on the noose and the hand forcing my arm up my back, pulled out of me, and flipped me over. My hands instinctively went to the leather noose around my throat, but he backhanded me across the cheek, grabbed both of my wrists, and forced my arms above my head, flat on the bedspread.

Moving his heavily muscled body up onto the bed, he straddled my chest with his knees and shot his load in three prodigious spurts on my face and chest.

"Not done, yet," he growled. "Open to it, bitch." He pushed his hard cock at my lips and, with a whimper, I opened my mouth and took it inside. He wasn't kidding. Four strokes to the back of my throat and he let off another load.

"Clean it," he demand, and I sucked the cum off his cock and coughed as he pulled it out of my mouth. In one swift move, he let loose of my wrists, slipped the belt off my throat and reached down and gave both of my nipples a cruel twist. I yelped, and he laughed.

I made to rise when he came off me, but he backhanded my face again, snapping my head to one side and making me fall back onto the bed with a groan.

"Stay right there, bitch. I might want to use you again. That was good. Enjoyed it. You like it like that, don't you?"

I whimpered some form of answer, croaking, my throat feeling like it had been crushed.

"What's that? Can't hear you."

"Yes," I managed in a gravelly voice. "I like it like that. I loved it."

"You love it and want it again. Say it."

"I loved it; want it again." I meant it.

"I know you did—know it's what you like. Came like Niagara Falls." He picked up his jeans, briefs, and T-shirt and padded out of the room. To shower, I assumed. There was a hall bath, but he could have used the one off my bedroom. Maybe he didn't know it was there, though, the door to it wasn't obvious. Like most everything in this house on a bluff overlooking a marshland running down to Coinjack Bay, it had been added on over the decades as an afterthought. The house was appropriately named Haphazard.

He was right. I'd come more than once during the ordeal—and had come big. Overall I'd have to describe it like that—an ordeal—though. Was it my fault that I loved ordeal, soared higher and came bigger from ordeal? Looked forward to the next, more cruel ordeal?

The man was an animal—and so strong and overpower. In his prime, a firefighter, probably half a decade younger than I was, I was sure. And on every level that seemed important, I'd enjoyed it immensely. There always seemed to be other levels, higher levels, though. And this firefighter I'd picked up was true to the form. Basically him saying he'd used me was spot on. A user. He was abusing me like this with no regard to my pleasure.

That I'd gotten pleasure out of it would bring him no pleasure.

I'd needed to get laid—and to get laid hard. I wouldn't have let him come home with me from the firehouse party in Maple if I hadn't. I'd had few illusions what he'd do to me; I'd sought him out. I'd gone there looking for just about what I got. A big bruiser of a man to take home and then take me hard. I even half knew it would be him—Chet.

I'd seen him before at Andy's, the gay-clientele tavern outside of Elizabeth City, some eighteen miles west, into the interior of northeastern North Carolina. And I knew he'd seen me there too. We'd spoken in passing—both of us working someone else at the time, and he'd dropped that he lived and worked in Maple. I'd said I didn't live far from there, on a bluff above the coastal marshlands on the west side of Coinjack Bay, separated from the Atlantic Ocean by the Outer Banks.

I'd checked around, which didn't take long in a small town like Maple, and found out that his name was Chet and that he worked part-time as a carpenter and part-time as a fireman—that his family lived in Elizabeth City, his father a prominent real estate lawyer there. I could believe the fireman part. He was a bodybuilder type. And all blond sunny looks. It scared me just to look at the hulkiness of him. And it aroused me.

I'd seen a guy stumble out of the back rooms at Andy's once, all sloppy grin, despite a black eye, and walking like he couldn't keep his legs together. Shortly he was followed out of the back by Chet, who was still tucking his T-shirt into his tight jeans and pulling his zipper up. It sent my blood boiling then—and in the weeks of running the image through my mind later. My fantasies focused more on the sloppy grin, the stumbling gait, and the bulge in Chet's crotch. The fantasy of him pulling that zipper down for me.

And when I brought him home today I hadn't been laid in a month or more.

A week before that I got one of those "gimme" calls soliciting support for the local fire department. I started into the regular "send me something in the mail; I don't entertain telephone solicitation."

"But this is the only call for money we do. We need the support, and we're the only fire station that could get to your house before it burned to the ground. Did I tell you that a contribution gets you an invitation to a firemen's party at the Maple firehouse the Saturday after next?"

The image of Chet, who I'd just found out was a Maple fireman, flooded into my brain, although I didn't know it at the time. I said I'd contribute and gave them a credit card number—all, I thought at the time, because I had been guilted—or maybe I realized that they were right. If there was no firehouse in Maple, my place didn't stand a chance in a fire. There weren't more than 25,000 people in the whole county, but we had to have a fire department. My rattletrap of a rambling wooden house clinging to a bluff was as likely to burn as anyone's—more likely probably. If I didn't contribute, who would?

I didn't even intend to go to the party at that point. It only occurred to me to do so when the ticket came in the mail—and, yes, after I'd connected this with the fireman Chet I'd seen come out of the back rooms at Andy's pulling his zipper up, a smug look on his face, and preceded by a scared rabbit with a hobbling gait and a black eye.

Chet was there, at the party. He saw me. He was looking magnificent in an athletic T, cut down to "here" both in the armholes and the neck, showing his bulging tanned chest and taut nubs, and wearing low-rise, tight jeans, rubbed to a lighter color over his basket. After a while, he sauntered over to me.

"I'm dying for a smoke. You are too, I think. Dying for something, I would guess. You're Rob Preston from out at that choice slice of land in the marshlands on the bay, aren't you? The book illustrator, I'm told."

God, he'd checked me out too. I was trembling just being near him. He towered over me. His chest seemed to be as broad as I was tall. The nipples were plump, full; his basket was straining at the material. I could clearly follow the line of him down his left thigh. And the muscles on the dude . . . he could easily break me in two.

And maybe he might do that if I asked him nicely. God, I missed Jesse.

"That's me, yes."

"And I've seen you at Andy's, over near Elizabeth City, haven't I?"

"That was me too," I said, although I think it may have come out as more of a squeak than anything else. He certainly was direct. "I've seen you there too."

"I saw you with Jesse, the black guy who moved down to Florida?"

"Yes, I've been there with Jesse."

"He's a power top."

"Yes he is," I answered, trying to keep my eye contact as level as Chet's was. And right there was why I hadn't been laid for a month. Jesse had moved to Florida and I hadn't found anyone new yet. Certainly not someone who would do what Jesse did. When Chet had seen me at Andy's, Jesse had been all over me, so Chet didn't have to do much figuring to know what was what about me.

"As I heard it, Jesse was into some real kinky shit. And was a rough fucker."

"Think I heard that as well." I sustained the direct eye contact.

"It's quiet and dark behind the firehouse. I'm dyin' for a smoke. You want to come with me?"

"I . . . don't smoke. Sorry."

"But you want to come with me anyhow, don't you?"

He was right. It was dark behind the firehouse. He also was right that he needed a smoke. He held me against the back wall of the firehouse with just one hand planted in my chest, while he leaned away from me and smoked his cigarette, giving me the evil eye the whole time. His T-shirt was gone; he had the torso of a serious bodybuilder.

"I could break you in two," he said from out of the blue.

"Yes, you could," I answered, trying to hold the level gaze into his eyes.

He nodded his head and smiled, like I'd just rubbed Aladdin's lamp the right way or something.

When he tossed the cigarette aside, I remember wondering if it still had a flame in it and whether he, a fireman, even cared that he had tossed it into brush. But it was too dark to know, and I didn't have time to think much about it. The cigarette gone, he came in close, shucked my T-shirt over my head in one swift move and pulled me into an embrace, his hands palming my back to press my groin into his. Neither of us could have been surprised to find the other one was hard.

His lips were on mine even before he'd exhaled the last puff of smoke, which he transferred to my mouth cavity. I wanted to cough, but he was kissing me so brutally that I couldn't. My eyes watered as the smoke swirled down into my throat. I did let loose a gagging cough when he released my mouth.

"It'll be like that," he muttered, still apparently seeing if I'd scare off.

"Yes," I answered. Yes, both to the realization I knew it would be like that and to the question of whether I wanted it like that. I'm sure he fully understood my acquiescence. Already asserting dominance over me; already understanding I was bowing to it.

He gripped my wrist behind my back and jerked it up painfully. As I yelped, he took my lips with another brutal kiss. I opened my mouth cavity to him immediately, gagging on his penetrating tongue.

"You want it like that," he declared when we came out of the kiss.

"Yes, I want it like that," I answered.

Assured I was completely cowed, he released my arm at the same time he released my lips and ran his hand up and down my naked back.

"Your back. Those welt lines?" He was grinning a knowing grin.

"They're mostly healed," I whispered. It had been more than a month since Jesse's farewell party at my house—just the two of us. Jesse had been at his cruelest.

Chet laughed and slammed me against the firehouse wall. He had grasped the wrist of my left hand and slammed it against the wall overhead. He moved the other hand to my crotch and explored and squeezed. Coming out of another kiss, I yelped at that, the crushing pressure on my balls, but he just possessed my mouth again. He let loose of my crotch and grabbed my right wrist, forcing my hand between us and to his crotch so that I could get the measure of him. He was harder; so was I. I gasped, and he let loose of the kiss and laughed.

"Climb me," he growled. With his free hand he lifted and bent my left leg so that it was hooked on his hip. Getting the idea, I lifted the other leg myself to his other hip. Then he pushed me up and down the wall with his pelvis, only the material of our jeans separating his crotch from my perineum. If we'd been naked, we'd be fucking.

"We still gonna do this?" he asked. Giving me every chance of an out.

"Yes."

He smiled a sneery smile. "You got somewhere we can go?" he asked in that deep-throated growl he was using. "Might not want to see what I have at home yet."

"Yes, my place, out on the bay."

"You're a real pretty boy. Great bod. I'm gonna fuck your lights out. Gonna punish you. Gonna break you."

"Yes." It had been a long time.

I did have a place to go, and he did fuck my lights out. And he did punish me. Not like Jesse could do, though. But it was early days.

He followed me home in his jeep. He seemed to know where he was going. I didn't even have time to close the front door of my house before he was manhandling me back to my bedroom, stripping us both, putting me on my knees, thrusting his dick in my mouth, grabbing my hair, and pulling my head back and forth on his rod. Then slamming me on the bed and assaulting me.

There was no better term for it. He assaulted me. It was all him getting what he wanted. I can't say I didn't get what I wanted along the way, though. And it wasn't rape by any means. It may have looked that way. It may even have felt that way to me, although that was all to the good of what I was in want of. But there was no question that I had asked for it—that I had agreed to it.

I lay there on the bed, panting, stroking my throat, and looking up at the thick floating beams in the raised ceiling of the bedroom, as I heard him pad around the house. I was waiting for him to come back. He had said he would if he felt like it.

"And you'll want it if I do you again, won't you?"

"Yes," I squeaked.

My legs were bent and open. I'd moved a pillow under the small of my back. I told myself that it was because if—no, when—he came back, I needed to be as open and at as good an angle for that monster of a cock he had that I could be. My thoughts went to the guy who had stumbled out of the back of Andy's. I could well understand now why he hadn't been able to put his legs together.

I also, subconsciously, at least, understood my interest in Chet, I guess. All that shit Jesse had done to me. One gets addicted to it. Chet did it a lot different than Jesse did, though. But they both got me very high and got me off very big.

He did come to the bedroom door once, a beer bottle in his hand, and say, "Geez, that was nice, Ron. You're a real good lay. Take it like a champ. Nice hole. Tight. But I reamed it real good, didn't I? You're carved for Chet's needs now." He withdrew, not waiting for a reply, which came in the form of a deep moan anyway. And, to my embarrassment, I felt disappointment.

After thirty minutes of quiet, I got off the bed and padded out to the living room, dining room, den, work room, and kitchen, all of which radiated off an entrance hall at strange angles. The front door was still open, there were two empty beer bottles on the kitchen island, and Chet was gone.

Again, I could have kicked myself, but I was a bit sad and disappointed. The fuck was brutal. But I'd set myself up for it, it was a totally fulfilling fuck, and I hadn't been laid in weeks. Would I see him again? Was that really my choice? Everything he'd said indicated there would be a repeat—and that it wouldn't be my choice.

I didn't want to think about it anymore. I had an appointment with my lawyer in Maple in the morning, followed by a tennis match with my parents' old friend, Avery Jameson, who'd been after me to sell my land to developers. I needed to get to sleep. In the morning I'd go into town. I'd pretend nothing happened here tonight. I'd probably be hobbling, though. I hoped I'd recovered before my first serve of the doubles tennis match at the golf club.

It occurred to me as I moved toward the bathroom off my bedroom that I needed to check on whether I had a black eye. There had been enough pain in general that I probably wouldn't have specifically noticed being given one.

All the time I was driving to Maple in my pickup the next day, the line of a song kept running through my mind: "Some will want to use you; some will want to be used by you."

Story of my life.

* * * *

"It's a lot of money, Ron. I really think you should consider it."

"I'm not selling to a developer, Larry," I answered. "I think I've made myself clear about that. And it isn't because of the house. It's the marshland. Too much of the coastal marshland is being destroyed. Virginia Beach and Norfolk are inching too close to us from the north. My mom and dad were friends of your parents. Our families spent a lot of time together. You know how my mom and dad felt about preserving the environment. Wipe out the marshlands around here and we can kiss our local wild life and plant species good-bye. I won't be any part of that."

"God, that's one raspy voice you got this morning, Ron. Caught a cold or something."

"Something that just came on," I answered, in embarrassment, as I rubbed my raw throat, a souvenir from the fireman the night before. "Woke up with it this morning."

Larry Heger—my lawyer, and the son of my parents' lawyer—sighed from across the window booth at the café in Maple and took a swig of his coffee.

Larry and I had gone to high school together in this town and been on the same district-winning football team. He'd been into bulking up and went on to the University of North Carolina on a football scholarship. I'd been fast enough for high school football but not big enough for collegiate ball and had gone to Duke's art school, keeping up with sports, but going more to tennis and track. Larry had taken on the craze of some form of Japanese martial arts that I couldn't pronounce, so he had remained in superb shape.

We'd been good friends. Almost too good. Going to different colleges either saved us from something or was a personal "ships passing in the night" tragedy. He was a user. Even that early in life I'd have let him use me if he had shown the slightest hint of wanting to. He was into using the cheerleader squad, though.

There had been rumors about him and men at college; there hadn't been a hint of anything in high school, or I might have made a move while he was doing his date in the front seat and me mine in the backseat after the senior prom.

With me at Duke, it was a fact, not rumors. But neither of us had openly or privately discussed anything about those options when we were in high school. He'd married, settled down in his father's law practice, and had more kids now than I could name. I had remained single and unattached—which meant I hadn't gotten beyond one-night stands very often. Jesse had been an exception, but we just met for sex; we didn't hang out with each other socially.

"It's good to have you back in the area, Ron," Larry said, leaning in toward me over the booth table. "We should go out and toss the ball a bit when football season comes around again—just for old time's sake."

"I didn't think I'd ever come back," I answered. "But I guess the pull of the beach and marsh was too much."

He sat back in the booth. "You always seemed to meld well with this place. There's been more than once that I would have liked to be somewhere else—a bigger city, maybe." He laughed then. "I guess anywhere is bigger than Maple. But more adventure in life, I guess. And speaking of marshes, I do remember how deeply your parents thought about preserving the marshes. But it's not like your piece of land is going to stand a chance of fighting that battle. The developer has the parcels on either side of you. He's already built a house for himself right at the top of the beach on the parcel to the south of you. He's here to stay. Your land, with that big flat area at the top of the bluff is right in the center of his plans—and it's prime location for developing."

I blew on my coffee. They sure made it hot and strong at the café. I needed something to loosen me up this morning. The firefighter from last night had worked every bone in my body. Quite a bone he had on his body too.

"I'm thinking of putting Haphazard in the land trust, Larry. Maybe even make a park out of it. It may be a losing battle on protecting the environment of the marshlands at

69

the edge of the bay, as you say. But at least there would be my chunk of land to show what once it was like."

"The land trust?" Larry hissed. "Keep your voice down when saying that word around here, Ron. In case you haven't noticed, this area is depressed as hell economically. The development down the bay is the best revenue stream we've seen in decades. You go saying you might put that land of yours in the trust and you'll need to start sleeping with a gun under your pillow at night. I won't press you further on selling the land—there will be plenty around here that will stand in line to do that—but I won't draw up a land trust application for you either. I'll recommend a good lawyer in Elizabeth City for you if you decide to go that route."

"Just said I was thinking about it, Larry. You say the developer has built a house for himself right on the beach line south of me? Didn't anyone around here tell him about hurricanes? And we're entering hurricane season. And how did he get it through the zoning process?"

"You know how he got approval through the system here, Ron. And you can't tell these guys from up Virginia Beach way about hurricanes and beach houses, Ron, but if it's not going to change their ways up at Virginia Beach, I don't think it will make much of a dent on their thinking down here."

"But it won't be just the environment that's ruined if they build down near the beach, Larry. Their houses won't last more than a couple of years anyway."

"You're preaching to the choir on that, Ron. But that's what he wants Haphazard for. He can fit a lot of house on that high land you have above the bluff."

"But that won't stop him from filling in the marsh and building down there too, will it?" I said, as I stood and tossed money for the coffee plus a tip on the table. "Sorry, I've got a tennis date to go to. You don't need to listen to any more offers on the land. I'm not selling. Nice having coffee with you, though. We should do this more often."

"Hope you win the match. Playing with Avery Jameson again?"

"Yeah. But it'll be doubles. Avery will get the tennis pro to partner him and he says he's invited a new guy who has joined the club to be my partner."

"So, he's loaded the deck by taking the pro for himself."

"Well, I did play on a nationally ranked collegiate team when I was at Duke, Larry. I didn't spend all my time there learning to draw pretty pictures to put in books. You could say that Avery just wants to even the odds. And I don't really care who wins the match. It will just be good to be swinging the racket again. It'll be my first time this spring."

"Oh, I think Avery will let you win—this time."

"Why's that?" I had started to back off from the table, but that brought me back. Larry stood then.

"Here, I'll walk you out," Larry said. He continued on. "Avery's one of the backers of the development. I'll bet he asked you to play today just to pitch you to sell. You can expect to have a lot of that coming to you from different directions."

"Thanks for the tip," I said, as we moved toward the café entrance.

"And watch your back, Ron. The longer you hold out the dirtier they're going to play."

"So, you're saying that developers can be as bad as lawyers?" I asked, as we got to the door.

We both laughed at that. Larry's laugh rang a little hollow, though.

Larry opened the driver's door of a fancy little sports car parked in a handicapped spot right in front of the café entrance. I said nothing about where he'd parked—Larry had been like that in high school too. But I'd just written it off then—but I couldn't overlook the car, which looked out of place in a town ruled by pickup trucks. Even I was driving a pickup truck.

"Nice wheels, but what is it?" I asked.

"It's a Crossfire. Made by Chrysler. But they don't make them anymore. I'll bet I have the only one in Northeast North Carolina. Sort of out of place in this town, isn't it? But I'm a toy guy, as you probably know." He paused here and looked at me, but then smiled and went on. "This is about the only excitement I get in my life."

"What, with three kids under seven?"

"I've got four kids. And especially with four kids under seven." We both laughed.

I waved him away. Larry sure had his quirks, but high school buddies are high school buddies. And he was a damn fine lawyer, I thought.

Sure enough, as Larry predicted, Avery and the tennis pro let me and my partner win the tennis match. The two of them combined were better than the two of us combined. The fourth guy, a well-muscled, impressively in-shape, distinguished, well-heeled businessman type who was introduced to me as Jack Dorsey, was good—especially for his age, which seemed to be mid forties—but he vied with Avery as the least capable of the four. His shortfall had to be training, not athletic talent.

I was rusty, but I still competed well with the tennis pro. It didn't take a whole lot of tennis winning for a pro at a rural country club like we had in Maple to qualify for the job. He mainly had to look real good for the ladies of the club, which Tony did.

Larry also was right that Avery pitched me at every change of side about the development. At these times, Dorsey and the tennis pro would talk to each other about the amenities of the club that Dorsey had just joined. But Dorsey also was eyeing me.

I couldn't help to take looks at him too. He was built big and solid and obviously worked out regularly. He had a mean, strong backhand on the court too.

The furtive looks continued in the shower and locker room too. I couldn't help noticing that he was hung like a horse and looked even better built in the nude than in tennis togs. The smooth businessman look he'd exhibited on the court earlier turned slightly, but purposely, I thought, to something a bit wilder and more thuggish in the nude— when we were both in the nude and in the communal shower. Maybe it was the mean-looking tattoo of really thorny brambles encircling his right bicep, I thought. The chunky chain-link necklace and black mesh bikini briefs he put on before dressing into a tailored suit that returned him to the businessman look enhanced the "something else altogether" aura of him.

The looks he was flashing at me were ones of interest—I'd been cruising enough not to mistake that. He put an arm around my shoulders as we were exiting the shower and reaching for towels and brought both his body and his face close into mine. I was somewhat embarrassed, because I was half hard by the time. So was he.

"Enjoyed getting to partner with you today, Ron," he said to me, with a smile. "I had to wheedle at Avery to get us introduced. Wouldn't mind partnering and playing with you again soon. Would like to get to know you and discover what you like—and maybe share with you what I like. Maybe we could catch a drink somewhere sometime. I've heard that Andy's over near Elizabeth City is a good place. A black guy named Jesse told me it was a good place."

The shock at how directly he was declaring himself— and categorizing me too—and especially with us both in the nude, half hard, sent me stumbling into the locker room. I felt the sting of his hard slap on my rump and a hearty laugh from behind me as I moved.

Nothing more was said—everything was in looks at each other—and at how both of us had gotten harder as we went to our individual lockers in the same row. If there hadn't been other men wandering around the locker room,

I'll bet he would have tried to fuck me right there on the wooden bench between the rows of lockers.

And I would have let him. I would have spread my legs, opened up, pulled the big cock inside me, and moved my ass for him. The disturbing aspect, since I'd take dominating sex anywhere I could get it, was how much he assumed—that he assumed I'd be easy. But I guess that was a key aspect of the kink. The dominator knew what he could have, and the sub was easy for it.

He'd made no bones about doing a full frontal to me as he folded his package into the mesh briefs. Although the tennis pro, Tony, cut an arousing figure in the shower too, there was a world of difference in how he and Avery—who was nothing to write home about in the body department—related to me in the locker room shower and how Jack Dorsey did.

The possibility didn't escape me that Avery might have found out about my proclivities and brought Dorsey in to soften me up sexually to a deal on my land, but, as Dorsey made no move to go with me anywhere right after tennis, I told myself that I was still running on a high from the rough fucking the fireman, Chet, had just given me and that Dorsey wasn't going to be as pushy.

"Later," he said gruffly, as, dressing quickly, I was able to leave the locker room before he was fully dressed.

I didn't think about that again until later in the day.

* * * *

After tennis I was a bit spaced out and, despite, or because of, the previous night, a little keyed up sexually, so I went home to contemplate. There was work to do—illustrations for a gay Kama Sutra book a publisher was doing—and I was in the mood for such work. I diddled around with that for an hour after I got home, but that didn't lessen my tension, so I went into my bedroom, opened the

74

bottom drawer of my nightstand, pulled out the Fleshjack I kept there—a "realistic experience" foam-lined masturbation aid I kept for emergencies such as this—and worked myself while thinking of Chet from the previous night, the sensuality and interest that this Jack Dorsey I'd just met exuded, the issue of the marshland, the developer who wanted to destroy it, and all of the people in Maple who supported him.

"Fuck it," I muttered after I'd relieved myself. I didn't feel like going back to the illustrations, though, so I grabbed a couple of beach towels, slipped on flip-flops—the only clothing items I was wearing—and headed down to the beach. I had my private slice of Coinjack Bay beach below the bluff and across a wide expanse of marshlands that my parents had built a wooden walkway over in as unobtrusive manner to the natural setting that they could manage. I had the luxury of swimming and sunning in the nude.

I powered out beyond the surf line and swam laps back and forth over the expanse from one end of my property line to the other. I saw the wooden monstrosity on stilts the developer had built down at the beach line on the south side. He'd left a good bit of the marshland around the house untouched, but it would only be a matter of time until what he'd done would destroy the ecosystem there and leave him with a rotting, smelly mess. And then to the north I saw that the marshlands had already been bulldozed and that landfill dirt was being brought in to raise the land a couple of feet and level it for the coming house development.

Frustrated and angry, I swam back to my own beach and lay on my back, with an arm thrown over my eyes to blot out the intruding world of "progress." I was panting lightly. The swim had been exhausting. At one time it would have been cleansing too, but that was before I saw with my own eyes what was happening at either side of my property.

I think it was the feel of the change in the sun beating on my body that made me pull the arm away from my face and look toward the sun. The very-nicely cut body of Jack

Dorsey—the naked body of Jack Dorsey—crouched down on his haunches beside me and looking down at me was putting me in shadow. A horse-hung cock swung between his spread knees, reaching for the ground, but that was hardening up even as I watched it. I jerked to full consciousness and started to sit up.

"No, don't. Lay there like that. Your body is gorgeous stretched out like that." He placed a palm on my belly, as if that would hold me in place. Psychologically it worked. I stayed where I was, feeling myself start to pant shallowly again, my cock beginning to rise. He already was in full erection in the time between I'd opened his eyes and he'd spoken, his beefy balls hanging low between his spread thighs.

He was wearing the thick chain-link necklace and now I could see that there was a medallion hanging from it—a heart shape with crossed rods behind it. One a whip and the other a phallus. On a scrolled ribbon across the heart was the word "Daddy." I let out a moan.

"We set up what was going to happen between us back in the club locker room, right? That I'm going to do you?" he asked in a low, strong voice.

"Yes, I guess so." When he put it that way, a dominator's command, all I could do was agree.

"You're going to let me play with you, aren't you? Rough. Jesse rough. I'm going to be your daddy and you're going to be my bad boy, needing to be punished. Am I wrong?"

"No, you aren't wrong," I whispered. His hand had moved down to encase my cock and he was stroking it. I arched my back to him and ran my hand up his arm to that thorny tattoo encircling his bicep.

"Yes, that means what you think it means," he growled.

He leaned over for a deep kiss, which ended in him taking my lower lip between his teeth. He lingered there a long moment, the anticipation building up in me, before he bit down, drawing a bit of blood. I yelped. And then I yelped again when he dipped his face to my chest and bit a nipple. All the time his hand was stroking my cock.

"It means what you think it means," he repeated.

"Where did you come from? How did you know where I lived?"

"Avery told me where you lived. Interesting house you have up on the bluff. You'll have to show it to me."

"Yes," I answered with a whimper.

"I'd heard rumors about you. Jesse bragged about what he did to you, what you took. I asked Avery to introduce us. You don't mind, do you?"

"No," I answered in a whisper.

"I'm going to make you come now."

"Yes. Please."

He moved over my body in a 69 position and took my cock in his mouth. I was uncut; he cut. I went straight to sucking on his bulb, while he played with mine by running his tongue under the foreskin and rimming the bulb—and listening for me to yip yip as he teethed and bit on the rim of the foreskin. Soon, though, my cock had filled out to where the foreskin pulled back from the bulb of its own accord, and he went to deep-throating me and sucking on the bulb, forcing the tip of his tongue into my piss slit.

"You ever been sounded?" he asked.

"No."

"Well, well."

A shiver of fear and anticipation ran up my spine.

I gave up on sucking his cock and threw my head back, looking directly up into the sky, mouth yawning open and groaning deep in my throat as he relentlessly pistoned my shaft in his mouth and reached under a thigh with one of his hands to get a good grip on my balls, lacing them in his fingers, distending them, crushing them.

I writhed under him, trying to pull away, begging him for mercy and relief and screaming to the sun, setting off sea gulls to reel about overhead and harmonize with me, but he was too strong for me and held me tightly. My testicles tried to withdraw into my sac in preparation for an ejaculation, but he followed them up into the sac with probing, pinching fingers. With a cry, I shot my load in his mouth.

Holding the wad of cum there, he quickly reversed on my body, still holding me in an embrace and went into a kiss that shared my cum between us. I was whimpering from the assault and also from the relief.

"You didn't come," I whispered when I was able to. "Sorry, I couldn't continue—"

"I want you to show me your house. Then I'll come. You'll come again too. Multiple times."

"Yes. Yes, of course," I answered.

He was sitting on the edge of my bed when I came out of the bathroom, where I'd showered and taken the time to clean myself out. There wasn't much question what was coming—what had me keyed up was not knowing how it would be done and what would accompany it. Could he possibly be as cruel as Jesse and Chet were in their own ways?

When Jesse had gone, I thought that the kinky sex phase of my life that Jesse had refined was over. He wasn't the first one to take me in a manner that heightened my release, but he had been the cruelest one by far. Northeast North Carolina was such a backwater, and I hadn't found anyone even close to Jesse's style at Andy's. It had been more than a month of drought. Although offers were frequent, Jesse had tuned me to certain needs. Was that hiatus what made me fall so easily into it again?

Jack was giving me a sloppy grin as I emerged from the bathroom. He held the Fleshjack from my nightstand in his hand. And he'd found and pulled out the restraints at the four corners of my bed that had been tucked under the mattress—the ones that only Jesse and I had used before.

"Shall we play?" he asked in a mocking voice.

The first time we both came—almost simultaneously—Jack was sitting on the side of the bed, with me crouched in his lap, facing him, my legs bent, my feet being used for leverage to rise and fall, him supporting the small of my back as I was cantilevered over the bedroom rug, my hands dangling at my side. Our cocks locked together inside the Fleshjack, the rods stretched alongside and throbbing against each other, and Jack stroking it down as I stroked up into it, his cum mingling with mine when we both had ejaculated.

"Ever been double penetrated?" he whispered.

"No."

"My, my, we have such a lot of new games to play."

Chills up my spine again. Panting. Was he going to be as cruel as Jesse, just in different ways?

After a rest in the kitchen, where I drank beer and Jack drank bourbon with a, "Sorry, I don't drink beer," we returned to the bedroom and to the restraints at the corner of the bedposts.

Jack was under me, sitting up. I was in his lap, all four limbs restrained and stretched out toward the four corners of the bed. His cock was up inside me, deep and churning. One of his arms embraced my chest, rubbing across clips he'd attached to my nipples, making me gasp and groan. The hand of the other arm held my cock captive in the Fleshjack, which he was pumping vigorously up and down on my cock. He'd found the ball gag in my nightstand, and I was huffing and puffing and sounding off around that as I could, my neck resting on his shoulder, my eyes glued to the freestanding beams overhead, as he bent his face down and bit down the side of my neck and onto my shoulder.

I came in great globs of cum over and over again. So did he, deep inside me, filling me with his cum—barebacking me. Both of us living on the arousing edge.

He released me from the restraints and we lay stretched out against each other, me in his close embrace.

"Tell me that was good for you."

"That was good for me," I answered. "Hadn't had that in too long. I don't know, guess I need the intensity, the lack of control." Had Jesse ruined me for more normal sex? I wondered. One thing was for sure, it helped me in drawing my special collection book illustrations. The porn publishers were coming to me for all their kinky sex illustrations. Positions I could draw, because I'd been in them. I knew what expressions to put on the model's face.

"Call me Daddy," he growled, as he reached down, laced my balls between his fingers, and squeezed.

"Oh, God. Oh, shit."

"Do it. Call me your daddy. Tell me you love this."

"I love this, Daddy. Oh, fuck! Fuck, fuck, fuck!"

"You're my bitch. Say it."

"I'm your bitch!" He released the pressure and turned away from me, putting his hand in the lower drawer of my nightstand, coming up with linked wrist restraints.

"We're going to have a lot of fun, you and I. You're going to be my bitch and I'm going to beat you down to where you'll do anything I want." He had pulled my arms around to my back while he said this and put my wrists in the restraints.

"Anytime, anywhere I want it, bitch. Say it."

"Anytime, anywhere you want it, Daddy."

I was exhilarated. A replacement for Jesse. Not as cruel as Jesse . . . yet. But it was early days.

He lay on his back. His erection had returned. "It's time for you to take care of me again. I want you to ride my cock. Tell me you want to ride my cock."

"I want to ride your cock, Daddy."

80

He pulled me onto his lap, straddling his hips, facing him, screwing my channel down on his hard cock again, my wrists bound behind my back. I started riding the cock in churning back and forward, side to side, revolving motions. He raised his torso to me, grabbed my butt cheeks—squeezing them, separating them, kneading them in the same motion I was making in riding his cock. Slapping them, digging his claws into them.

He took my lips in his, brutally kissing me. biting my lower lip when pulling out of the kiss. Laughing at the yelp that produced from me.

"Tell me you want me to punish you."

"I want you to punish me, Daddy." I whimpered. And, fuck help me, I did want him to punish me.

He laughed, leaned down, and chewed on my nipples, one after the other.

"Oh, fuck. Oh, shit. Oh fuck," I whimpered as his teeth chewed on my nipples, his claws dug into my butt cheeks, and I rode the cock, and rode the cock, and rode the cock.

An hour later, after he'd left me moaning on my back on my bed, the telephone on the nightstand rang.

"Hello," I answered groggily.

"Got you up?" Larry Heger asked cheerily.

"Already been up. Now I'm down again," I answered.

"Just wondered if Jack Dorsey had contacted you yet about upping the offer for your land."

"What? Who?"

"Jack Dorsey. He's the developer trying to buy your land—the guy who's built that pile of wooden crap on the beach to the south of you. He's offering four mil now."

"Son of a bitch," I yelled when I'd put the telephone down. "Interested in me, was he? I should have seen that coming. No way in hell that man's going to get my land—or anything else from me. Son of a bitch! Anything he wants me to do? I'm his bitch? Screw that."

But why did I feel I'd lost something I only now had refound?

* * * *

I spent the rest of the afternoon making telephone calls. I was talking to my financial manager—my parents had left me a healthy portfolio of stocks and I did well myself with the book illustrating—and various banks where I had accounts socked away. By an hour after dinner, I was cooled down enough and mellow enough from wine that I could return to working on my illustrations for an hour.

The wind is what first caught my attention. I went over and turned on the TV. A hurricane warning was running along on a band at the base of the screen. I turned that off and turned the radio on, which informed me that a hurricane I'd thought was on its way to Bermuda had taken a nasty turn to the west. It wasn't going to hit us here on the North Carolina coast directly, but it was going to brush close enough to whip anything into the air that wasn't anchored down.

Having everything anchored down outside was my mantra anyway. Patio furniture got moved out from a storage room when I wanted to use it and then moved back in. And the house had a low profile on the top of the bluff—a rambling one story, with berms around it to disrupt wind currents. There were no trees near the house, along the driveway, or even near the road running in front of my land. That was by design. We'd weathered more hurricanes on this property without any damage than I could count. The place looked like it was falling down, but looks were deceptive in this case.

As for the marsh, it thrived from the occasional passage of a hurricane.

Feeling safe, but knowing the electricity easily could cut out, I turned all of the lights off; unplugged the computers; took a long shower; hit the bed early, in the nude; used the Fleshjack to jack off and mellow out, and went to sleep, listening to the humming of the generator that backed up the power to the refrigerator and freezer.

I woke up in the middle of the night in bondage, only coming fully awake when a yoke rod was being set in place. It was totally dark. I heard no sound other than the howling wind clawing at the house. A man, obviously naked other than black gloves and a balaclava hood, was wrestling me into submission. He was bigger and stronger than I was. I knew it was a man because I could feel his erection poking at me as we struggled.

I was making a little progress, both of us breathing hard, me not wasting what breath I could muster in screaming or even trying to argue with him, because the howling wind made anything I could scream futile. But just to be sure he could control me, he hauled off and popped me one on the chin. While I was trying to recover from that, he put the yoke rod in place, my wrists trapped in fleece-lined leather restraints at the far ends of the bar and another leather collar around my neck.

When he'd turned me over on my belly and put a thigh spreader in place, I was almost entirely immobilized. He then attached leads going from the wrists restraints on the yoke rod down to the thigh spreader that forced me up onto my bent knees in a doggy fuck position. A lead going from the end of the yoke rod down under the bed and up to the other end of the rod and pulled tight held my cheek flat on the bed. A blindfold, that seemed a little excessive considering the darkness, although, granted, there was an occasional flash of lightning that would have given me some glimpse of the figure assaulting me if my mind was clear and my adrenaline wasn't pumping—which they were.

A ball gag completed the total incapacitation.

Then the ass work started. A dildo. A vibrator. His cock—a big, thick one. What writhing I was able to do in

83

that confinement was accentuated when he started with the dildo and his cock together.

He was mounted over me. I'd gone to sleep without putting the Fleshjack away, and while he rested between the first and second fucks, he moved his hand under my waist, holding the Fleshjack, and jacked me off with it. While he did that he licked the disappearing welts on my back and bit all over my back and up into my neck.

After hours of torment and fucking, a small vial of something came around to under my nose, I inhaled a pungent smell, and went out like a light.

When I woke, it was calm outside—and light. I was sore as hell, and felt cramped from the position I'd been bound in. But the toys were gone—except for the Fleshjack that was encasing my cock.

I gingerly rose from the bed and padded out to the living area. Nothing seemed amiss. I opened the refrigerator, suddenly in need a beer. But all my cold beer was gone. I say "all." I probably had been down to a six pack in there. There was more stashed out in the garage.

I went around the house looking for how he'd gotten in. One hallway went on forever, having two bedrooms and a bath on either side of the hallway and the garage at the end. There were patios on either side of the house there and all of the bedrooms had sliding glass doors out to the patio. In the last bedroom toward the land side, the sliding glass door was ajar. The carpet was soaked because rain water had come it. I'd attend to that later. When I tried to slide the door shut, I found it wouldn't latch. I'd have to get someone out to fix that too.

It was up for grabs whether this was how the assaulter had gotten in or if the storm had pulled a door with a faulty catch open.

Getting that fixed probably couldn't happen for several days, though. In looking outside, I could see that the hurricane had brought a lot of limbs and some trees down.

Since we had the trees well away from the house, there probably wasn't any structural damage here. But there would be damage elsewhere in the region, so fixing a sliding glass door wouldn't be much of a priority for workmen for a while.

I'd just have to live with it. I don't know who it was who had assaulted me in the night, but I had my candidates. It also had had me skipping along the clouds, so if this was some sort of warfare tactic to get me to sell the land, they were going to have to get a lot rougher than that.

It certainly wasn't something I could report to the police without resulting in more questions than answers.

It meant I should start activating my own plan, though, which would require me to go into town and see Larry Heger. The phones didn't work. Neither did the electricity, although my generator had kicked in to take care of the refrigerator and freezer. Cell phone coverage seemed to be out too.

Larry lived right on the edge of Maple, in a big plantation house that had been there since the early nineteenth century. He could walk to work even after a storm like this. But he lived close enough to work that I could walk to his house if he wasn't at his office.

He was about the only one in the area I could trust with my plan.

I went out and got into the truck and started driving toward town. I only got as far as the driveway into the land at the south of mine—the parcel owned by the developer who I now knew was Jack Dorsey. From the top of the drive into that parcel, I could see where fire trucks had tried to get in but had been stopped by two large trees that had fallen across the drive. An ambulance was there too. Beyond that, down toward Dorsey's beach area, I could see the column of smoke.

A hurricane had gotten his ill-placed wooden McMansion already. I parked the truck out of the way on the main road and walked into where the fire engines were parked. When I got to those, I was met by Chet, in full firefighter's gear, carrying the naked body of a young man—not Dorsey, I could tell at a glance. The young man was breathing and didn't look like he'd been burned, but he was unconscious. Other firemen and EMTs, the latter receiving the young man and moving him to the back of the ambulance, were milling around.

"Nothing we could do for the house," Chet told me, with a grin that indicated he enjoyed playing fireman—and probably had enjoyed carrying the naked body of the young man. I recognized him. He was a soda jerk at the town's drug store—a cute guy, barely twenty. Willowy, but obviously effeminate, limp wristed to the max. Too obviously queer and delicate for me.

"The wind was too strong for the structure and it was too exposed to the waves where it was," Chet said. "Shitty construction. Before the electricity went off lines came down and started a fire. The place is a wreck. No way should anyone have been permitted to put up a house like that there."

"The owner, Dorsey?" I asked.

"Already in the bus. Smoke inhalation. No burns, though. They were in the basement. But both of them will be in the hospital for a few days, learning to breathe again. Reinforced concrete, the basement room. Quite a setup down there. Better than my own chamber." Chet was grinning wide. "Lots of toys. The cutie was hanging from the ceiling. I liberated this. Thought we might use it."

All the time he was talking, Chet was holding up a yoke rod. One exactly like the one that had been used on me in the night. Maybe it was the same one. Fuck help me, my thoughts went immediately to Jack Dorsey. After resolving to have nothing more to do with him, what I was thinking now was that he really was into heavy-activity domination. My thoughts last night were that maybe this was just a persona he'd taken on to get to me, to make me bend to his will and sell him my land. But now? Shit help me, I was thinking of the possibility of hooking up with him again—when he'd gotten out of the hospital.

Even if he was the one who had assaulted me last night? Did I really want to answer that?

Chet was still talking. "Had half a notion to use the little honey myself where he was hanging. But he was gasping for air, and not in a controlled choke sex fun kind of way. Has left me horny, though. I'll have to hang him up somewhere when he recovers and give him what I would have liked to give him today."

"You have a chamber of your own?" I asked.

"Yep. You need to come over there—and come for me. We'd have a whole lot of fun. You'd come a lot." He laughed.

"And a hang bar?"

"Sure. A sling too. Nothing like all the shit this Dorsey guy had in his basement, though."

He held up the yoke rod again and wagged his eyebrows at me. "Let's let the other firemen clear out. Busy day. I'll do you right here. Pity the yellow tape is up and the structure ain't sound. We could use his chamber."

I was thinking again that maybe it *was* the same yoke from last night. If so, it was used on me twice within nine or ten hours. Chet stood there, grinning at me, as the ambulance and fire trucks got loaded with firefighters and pulled out onto the road. Chet, though, stood still, holding the yoke rod and smiling at me. A pickup truck was left when the dust settled by the departure of the other vehicles. His, I guess. He must have gotten the alarm when he was off duty and came over in his truck.

"Ain't got long, but that made me horny," he said. "Good thing you're here. March your pretty little ass over into those bushes over there. Strip as you walk."

For the second time that morning, I was on my knees, cheek to earth, incapacitated by a yoke bar, while Chet, in full firefighter gear, only his fly open, mounted my ass and rode me hard. He used my belt this time for reins, running the loop between my teeth, like a gag, and pulling hard back on that when he wanted my attention. Rode me like a cowboy, slapping my buttocks and commanding me to buck like we were in a rodeo ring while he plowed me.

When he let me up, he asked me where I was headed.

"Into Maple," I said. All I wanted at the moment, though, was a shower and a soft pillow to sit on.

"It'll be hard getting there for some time," he said. "The fire trucks had to use all sorts of back roads to make it. I suggest you stay at home. If you've got beer on ice, I might show up later and give you a good fucking." He winked at me.

So, I thought, just maybe you already did that last night.

I gave up on the day, though, and went back to my drafting table and made good progress on my current project. The electricity came back on about noon. I took that as a reminder and went out to the garage, brought in another six pack of beer, and put it in the frig. The telephones came back up soon thereafter. No one answered at either Larry's office or home, though, so I decided he must have taken his family inland the previous evening, in advance of the storm.

I was wrong about that, though. Larry called me at 5:00 p.m. and invited me over to the house for dinner.

"Sally says she doesn't want to chance refreezing the meat that was in the freezer while the electricity was off, so it's steak night for anyone who can show up. I'm told the roads are clear out your way now. Why don't you come in and join us?"

I was feeling the claustrophobia and I wanted to talk shop with Larry anyway, so I drove into town. I found him and a good many of his neighbors already plastered with beer

88

and sitting around the pool while the steaks cooked on several grills gathered in by the same neighbors. Larry saluted me with a beer and handed me one of my own.

"We got plenty of beer and steak," he said, slurring in words. "So life is good."

I'd obviously gotten there too late to consult with him on business—he was too far gone. But I enjoyed the dinner anyway, and begged off early, after coffee had been passed around a couple of times, saying I'd had a rough night during the hurricane—which I sure as hell had—and wanted to turn in early.

I went straight home and put in another two hours working on illustrations. I stopped when I realized that I was replicating the position and bondage restraints I'd been put in the previous night. Drawing them made me go hard, but most of them were of no use in a book on gay male Kama Sutra positions. "Fuck it," I said to the walls. I'd do an early night again—or try to.

If the guy who had assaulted me the previous night was Dorsey, as I suspected, I was safe now. He'd be in the hospital for a few days. By the time he was out, I'd have a surprise for him. And after today my plan had an even greater chance of working.

* * * *

The feeling of safety didn't last long.

I woke—briefly to a gloved hand over my face and that pungent smell at my nostrils again.

When I came to, I was hanging from a floating beam in the ceiling, fleece-lined wrist restraints extending my arms far apart on individual leads from the beam. I was dangling with my toes barely able to reach the bedroom carpet. My legs were held out wide by a stretcher extending from one ankle to the next. I couldn't see anything—I was blindfolded. I couldn't say anything—a ball gag was in place.

I could hear, though. Heavy breathing. And I could feel. He was running gloved hands all over my body, making me moan and go hard. He knelt in front of me and took my cock in his mouth, sucking it hard. Off and on, he pulled away and, with a laugh, he slapped my cock and I writhed within the confines of my restraints.

A gloved hand encased my balls and pulled them down. A ball stretcher was wrapped around the base of the sac, bunching my balls in one packet, which he patted and then crushed with his fist until I was writhing and screaming through the ball gag. Heavy weights were hung from the ball stretcher, distending my aching balls toward the floor. He patted the weights, sending them swinging back and forth, making me moan at the aching stretch of the balls.

Another slap of the cock, making me jerk and gasp, and then nipple clips, connected by a chain were being put in place. He pulled on the chain, pulling my nipples painfully away from my body. Eyes watering again, throwing my head back and screaming again through the ball gag to the ceiling. Pull. Release. Pull. Release. Enjoying my deep moans and groans.

Once again a slap of the dick and a squeeze of the balls.

Then the flogging began. "Dance for me," he growled in a low, purposely changed voice.

And I danced for him as well as I could, in the confines of the restraints, trying to get away from the lash as he flogged me. On the back, on the chest, on the thighs. On my cock and balls. Never with as much power behind it as Jesse had used. Never enough to leave the angry red welts that Jesse did that last night. But with enough stinging force to have me huffing and puffing, dancing, and writhing for him.

A laugh and then a slap of the cock, a squeeze of the balls. A pull at the nipple chain. And then another, and another.

Then the sound of a zapper. "Dance for me," he growled.

And I danced for him as he touched me, giving me an electric shock, with the tip of the zapper. On the buttocks, the thighs, lifting my feet, zapping the tender insoles. My upper inner thighs, giving me notice of where he was working toward. But then painfully jerking the nipple clips off, and while they still stung, zapping me on the nipples. On my cheek. Back to the upper inner thighs. My balls, causing me to writhe in agony. Again and again. Up under the ball sac on the taint. On the bulb of my cock, causing me to bite down on the rubber of the ball gag and almost slicing through it with my teeth.

As I hung there, sagging on the restraints, moaning deeply, the zapper entering my channel. Zap once, twice, three times.

Hanging and moaning.

Pulling the ball gag out and putting his mouth close to an ear.

"Tell me you want more."

"I want more."

"Tell me you want me to fuck you."

"I want you to fuck me, Daddy."

A laugh and the ball gag was reinserted.

Then and only then, he knelt in front of me, taking my cock in his mouth, a hand pulling down on the stretcher weights. Sucking me, sucking me, sucking me. When I was about to come, pulling out, slapping my cock, laughing. Then taking me in his mouth and, eventually, letting me cum.

I was released from the wrist restraints and just sank to the carpet, moaning.

"Liked that, didn't you?" he growled in my ear in the false voice he was using.

I mumbled something through the ball gag. But, dammit, it *had* sent me to a higher heaven. Like Jesse, but still not quite to the edges Jesse reached. Enough, though.

He'd released my wrists, but had immediately imprisoned them again. The yoke rod again. He didn't release the ankle extender.

I was manhandled to the bed and slammed on my back, the yoke hanging over the end of the bed—thus my head and hands there too. The nipple clips came back on and he'd shimmied his way under the ankle extender and on top of me. He worked a thick cock inside my channel and plowed me hard, one hand rhythmically pulling on the chain of the nipple clamps. I bucked with him, wanting him to come inside me. I came again, but he didn't. I thought he was ready to come, but he wasn't.

He pulled out of my ass, my cum dripping down my inner thighs; climbed off the bed; and came around to my head, where it was thrown over the end of the bed. The ball gag came out, but I had no time to say anything before a mouth cage was inserted, holding my mouth wide open. Holding it open for him to slide his thick cock inside my mouth and face fuck me. He came in big globs down my throat, making me sputter and gag.

I sensed the vial coming to my face that time, smelling hints of that odor before it reaching my face. I held my breath and pretended that I had inhaled whatever it was and that it had put me out. But it didn't. I got enough to be woozy, but I wasn't unconscious.

He puttered around the room, releasing my restraints—all but the blindfold—and gathering up his equipment.

I played unconscious.

Not more than two minutes after I was sure he'd left the room, though, I jerked the blindfold off and painfully rose from the bed. I went immediately to the spare bedroom, where the sliding glass door had been jimmied. He fooled me, though. He'd gone out the front door. I saw the taillights of his vehicle as he raced up my driveway, though—and some sense of the curve of the vehicle's back end.

After checking the refrigerator—sure enough the six pack I'd put in there earlier was gone—I went back to my bedroom and flopped down on the bed. I was panting shallowly, growling deep down in my throat, and going over what had happened that night. And I was smiling and hardening up again. I . . . just . . . couldn't help myself. I reached for the Fleshjack.

Whooie, I daydreamed as I lay on my back, working the Fleshjack up and down on my hard cock and moving my pelvis with the motion, I hadn't had a taking like those of the last couple of days since Jesse. I might not be lonely for him after all. But this being taken by surprise—and at night, when I should be sleeping—was wearing me out. Besides, if all the nighttime assaults were designed to scare me into selling my land, they could escalate into something else altogether, something beyond the kinky sex. Something potentially lethal.

* * * *

I slept then, exhausted. When I woke up, close to noon, I went straight for the telephone and called, first, the hospital, and then Avery.

"Avery, it's Ron. Are you Jack Dorsey's lawyer in these land deals? You're not? Can you tell me who is?"

He could and did. I whistled. With Dorsey out of the picture now as my midnight assaulter—he was in the hospital last night and, besides, he'd turned down the offer of a beer, saying he didn't drink beer—I'd thought who was attacking me, fucking me totally, was evident. Now I wasn't at all sure.

I checked the freezer and then dressed and drove into town, stopping at the firehouse.

"Is Chet here?" I asked as I entered the cavernous truck hall.

"Naw. He's off today's roster," the fireman who had come to see what I wanted answered. "Could be anywhere. Probably home."

"Can you tell me where he lives?"

"Sure," he answered. "You that artist guy out on the bay Chet's been telling us about?"

"Probably," I answered. Then with a sneery grin, the fireman told me how to find Chet's place.

"You looking for him for any particular reason?" the fireman, who was a Hispanic hunk and a half and who was stripped down to fireman's slick pants and shiny boots, held up by suspenders, was giving me the once over. I recognized that look. Were my wants that easy to see? Yes, I guess so for those who knew how to look for them. Would I lie under him if he told me he wanted to fuck me? Yes, if he made dominator demands. It's what subs did for dominators.

"Sure. I'm looking for him for a very special reason."

"I know some of Chet's special ways," he answered, with a grin on his face. "I can do Chet's specialties too. If he don't satisfy you, you just come on back, you hear? We got rooms upstairs—soundproof rooms. I got some nice toys. As good as Chet's got. And I got plenty of time on my hands if no fire flares up."

"Sure, maybe," I said, backing out of the hall. I wasn't kidding. The bruiser looked like a definitely rather than a maybe.

"Sure maybe or sure sure?"

"Sure sure." God, he was a hunk and a half.

I almost made it out of the firehouse.

"Wait," the firefighter hunk called out. The sound echoed in the hall. "On second thought, I think Chet said he'd be out of town until later this afternoon. We got time now. Come upstairs with me." He approached me. He was unzipped, had his cock out, and was cupping his balls and cock with a hand. His equipment was adequate to the task and went well with his muscular torso, the slick pants, the boots—the suspenders even.

"I don't think . . . ," I started to say.

"On your knees and suck it," he commanded.

I went down on my knees in front of him and took his cock in my mouth.

We didn't make it upstairs. He did me on the front seat of one of the hook and ladder trucks.

An hour later I went on to Larry Heger's office. He was in and welcomed me into his office. I sat across from him and gave him a level stare. He smiled back at me, all friendliness and "we've been pals since high school."

"What can I do for you, Ron?"

"Well, first of all, you can stop stealing my beer and steaks from my freezer, Larry. You didn't tell me that the beer I was drinking at your house and the steak I ate were from my kitchen."

He gave me a confused, dumb look and then it dawned on him what I was saying behind that and a cagier expression set in.

"You also didn't tell me that you weren't just my lawyer—that you were Jack Dorsey's lawyer on these land deals too."

"He offered you a fair price," Larry said, defensively—and, like any lawyer, he went straight to the money part of the conversation rather than to the more explosive, kinky sex assault part. I guess he was still scrambling for some lifeline of denial on that.

"Well, I've got a counteroffer deal for Mr. Dorsey, Larry. Seeing as how you represent him, you can go over to the hospital and push it down his throat. After his house burned to the foundations and everyone has seen what a bad idea it is for him to build houses there, his development deal isn't worth a plug nickel. You can tell him that, regardless, I'll give him $2 million for the land parcel to the south—the one with the ruins of his dream house on it—if he'll also put the

95

parcel on the north in the land bank. It's worthless for building now. The marsh there has been destroyed, but if they stop dozing now, it might come back in time."

"You got that kind of money, Ron?"

"Check me out. I'll give you numbers to call, people to talk to. You bet I've got that and more. But I'm not offering Dorsey a penny more. This is a good deal, and if you two put your heads together, you'll see that it is. Hell, I've got land over toward Elizabeth City. I'll give him $1 mil for this land and throw in the other land over there, which is ready for development, in the deal. I have my reasons not to wish Dorsey gone altogether. It's just the land on the bay—the marshland that we all should be protecting—that I want out of his hands."

"I'll see what I can do."

"If you don't want me to talk to Sally and your kids about your . . . extracurricular activities, Larry, I suggest you make Dorsey jump at the deal. And a personal tip to you, Larry: When you drive to a sexual assault, you really shouldn't do it in that distinctive sports car of yours."

I was getting out of my chair while I said that, and I could see that I'd gotten through to him on that point at last. He looked frightened. But I didn't want him to be frightened. I wanted him to dominate. And I didn't want him to stop torture fucking me.

"Ron. Look. You must know I've always wanted you. And when I learned through the mill at Andy's that you'd take what I liked. I just didn't want you to know that—"

"Well, we both know now. Don't worry, Larry. I want what you have to give—what you've given me the last two nights. I don't have any reason to talk to anyone as long as you give me what I need. I just want you to make an appointment for it. I need my regular sleep. And I want you to stop rewarding yourself with my beer. Oh, and when you talk to Dorsey, tell him it isn't because I want him to leave the area—that I'm perfectly happy about playing . . . tennis . .

96

. with him. I just don't want him fucking up the marshlands any more than he has already."

I left him with his mouth gaping open. I didn't have the slightest doubt he'd sell the deal to Dorsey—especially in light of the fringe benefits on offer.

One more stop, setting the third leg of the three-legged stool down.

I found Chet at home, dressed just in athletic shorts. His muscles were bulging and he had an enticing sheen of sweat on his chest.

"You found me," he said with a grin. "I was working out. Anything I can help you with."

"Were you talking straight when you said you had a chamber of your own? Hang bar and sling and what not?"

"You bet I did. Want to see it?"

"Yes, now please . . . if you're not too busy."

He grabbed one of my butt cheeks and squeezed hard as I preceded him down the basement steps. I wiggled my butt and sighed.

"Do you happen to have a set of sounding rods too?"

"Absolutely."

"And know how to use them?"

"You bet."

For the Glory of the Earth

Ervin Walker hiked up to the top of the ridge of the White Oak mountain range as he did every Friday afternoon, weather permitting. He was standing there, looking northwest over the rolling south central Virginia farmland as he had done nearly every Friday from mid afternoon until almost twilight for the past twenty-four years since he had received the call. This was his time to meditate and to let the words he would preach come Sunday morning at the Pentecostal chapel down in Pleasant Gap sink into him. Somehow standing here and looking down into the valley beyond his small farm, his own little slice of heaven, was what gave him his inspiration.

He had been born on this farm and he planned to die on this farm. Others were talking of selling, some because they just could not make a go of it anymore. But his land had come to his family at the time of their freeing, during the War of Succession, and each first son of each generation of the Walkers since then had pledged to remain on the land and to do their work for the glory of the earth. Nothing was more important than preserving the glory of the earth and receiving the bounty gleaned there from days of plenty and fallow alike. That they had received more than their usual share of days of fallow for too long now was one part of the

troubles on the land hereabouts, but only one part. It had been seven years. That meant something to Ervin, more apparently than to some of his neighbors who were close to giving up. He had the faith the seven years of famine would be followed by seven years of plenty. He lived by this knowledge, which had seen his family through many generations of troubles with the earth in the valley he now looked down into. His family had known to lay up a good portion of the bounty in the feast years to tide them over in famine years, and they thus far had managed thereby to hold a steady course.

Rain. What they needed was rain. And protection from the outside forces of evil that were descending on this valley. Ervin lifted his arms and looked heavenward, looking for signs of rain, praying for the rain. And, with a thought to the outside forces threatening the valley, he was also listening for that one word or phrase that always came to him late Friday afternoon. The word or phrase around which he would construct the simple message he would impart to the faithful few in his momma's chapel down in Pleasant Gap.

He stood there for more than an hour, eyes closed, denying himself the glorious sight of his own farm descending from the ridge into the valley below. Denying himself the sin of knowing how prosperous he was compared to many of his neighbors and how fortunate a man of color such as he was to have been from a landowning family these past hundred and fifty years and more. Pushing out the sin of pride—and closing his mind to the other sin, the most powerful of those that plagued him but that he could not withstand—he rocked his solid, muscular body of a man not quite fifty and used to working the land hard with honest, manual labor, and he hummed and opened himself to the word.

When the word came, it was a single word this time, not a phrase, as it often was. It was the word "sacrifice." It entered his mind so strongly, with a thunderclap that

99

tantalized, not promising rain, but marking the shift in fronts and the blast of dry heat, that Ervin knew this was the word he was meant to talk on Sunday morning. And it came to him with such strength that he knew that it was also the key to the valley's broader, more immediate problem. He didn't know how it was key to this, but he often didn't know the purpose of the word he was to preach while he stood on the top of the mountain range. Often fuller knowledge of what he was supposed to say and do came to him while he was doing his Saturday chores, working almost twice as hard on a Saturday as he did any other day of the week because there was to be no toil on Sunday. Sometimes the message didn't enter him until just as he was standing on a Sunday morning to let it out of him.

The word had come earlier than usual. It was still daylight when he descended to the split-rail fence line marking the inner yard around the house, where the smaller farm animals and the tractor and old Ford pickup were kept. As he approached the farm yard, he felt his insides tensing up and that old sin tearing at him. There was nothing he could do about that, though. He had tried, but he could not deny that no matter how much he prayed or attempted denial. There were more pressing matters before him; this was a sin so great that he would need that and just that to concentrate on—someday. And now the temptation was overwhelming.

He should never have taken Monte, Diamonte Moore, on. But when he had done so, that had been because of another call that came to him on the mountain top. The call that the young man needed his help, needed a chance to fulfill his own destiny.

But maybe it was a testing of himself, of Ervin Walker. If so, Ervin had failed the test. The young man was just too attracting—and, the real downfall, too willing, too pliable. He gave himself without question, with no fuss, no reproofs, just as if it was the most natural thing, when every fiber inside Ervin screamed out that it was not natural.

Ervin's eyes went to the young man as he approached the farm yard. Monte was at the wire fencing around the chicken house, on his knees and leaning over at the edge of the wire, repairing it where the chickens had pulled the wire out of the dirt at the base of the fence and nearly had it separated to the point where they could escape the pen, little knowing that the fence was there to protect them.

The older man ached, as he always did, at the sight of the young man's bare back. Nothing aroused the juices inside the man more than the sight of those young, broad, muscled shoulders. Monte had come to him as an outcast in his last year of high school up in Chatham, where he had withdrawn from the school football team, despite high school football being the end all of everything in this region of the state. The reason put out to the public was that Monte left the team because he was drawn to working the land and raising and caring for animals. His teammates and schoolmates had derided him and shunned him—not because he was not suited for football, because he had a magnificently formed body and a talent for the game, but because he would not devote his full time to it—and because of the rumors about what he had done with his body.

Monte also knew what none of his classmates or the school's alumni who were so taken up with the success of the football team knew for sure, although some suspected. Monte knew he couldn't spend time in the school's locker room with other young men without revealing the secret he himself had only learned shortly after his eighteenth birthday when the football coach, Mr. Docrity, had given him a ride home from practice one night and stopped on the banks of Green Creek in a remote location and fucked Monte four ways from Sunday in the bed of his Dodge Ram truck.

Monte hadn't struggled against the fucking. He hadn't minded it or questioned the coach; he'd just laid back in the bed of the truck and opened his legs for the coach to do what he wanted, locking eyes with the coach in a welcoming smile and no more than a moan and grimace and arching of his back and reaching around to grasp the coach's bare buttocks as Docrity's slowly entered him and began to pump, pumping away the young man's innocence and virginity.

This uncomplicated, full surrender of Monte to the coach's lust inflamed Docrity and caused him to come back again and again for what Monte willingly gave him.

After two months of football practice and long rides home by the coach, Monte's teammates had started to razz him about what he was giving the coach. Monte, uncomplicated in his sexuality, would have told they what he'd given the coach, but Docrity had forbidden him to do that. The young man had been too conflicted by the directions in which he was being pulled to remain on the team. And while withdrawing from the team, he'd withdrawn from most of the rest of life as well.

Withdrawing even from Chatham wasn't totally Monte's choice. As rumors spread of what the coach was doing with Monte, it was Monte who took the pressure. It had to be Monte who seduced the coach when he was overworked and vulnerable.

The coach had taken the football team to state semifinals four years in a row. It wasn't the coach who was going to be taken to task. And the coach wasn't going to stop fucking Monte by his own decision. Monte wasn't planning on giving up the coach either, but the second time he was taken into the shadows behind the school gym, beaten by his former teammates, and told to get out of town, he did so— as soon as he picked up his high school diploma.

Monte's shyness and ostracism had led his school counselor, a childhood friend of Ervin's, to approach Ervin about taking the boy in to explore his love for animal husbandry on a farm—a farm a good distance from Chatham—as soon as he finished school and until his classes at the community college in Danville, to the southeast, commenced. Little did the counselor know the temptation and perpetuation of an "issue" she was creating for both the young man and for Ervin.

She had never known why Ervin's wife had left him.

Ervin walked up behind the crouching Monte and placed a hand on the young man's shoulder. Having heard the older man approaching, Monte didn't flinch.

"I'm fixin' the wire so they can't peck their way out," he murmured.

"I see that you are, You're doing a fine job of it," Ervin answered in a low, hoarse voice.

Monte turned his head and looked up at the older man, a knowing look entering his eyes. Both of Ervin's hands were on Monte's bare shoulders and he moved them, gliding down to the young man's shoulder blades. The feel of the hard muscles on a young man's back was a fetish for Ervin, bringing out urges he couldn't resist. He stood back up, his knees now touching Monte's back, but stayed standing only long enough to unbutton his shirt and spread it apart. Then he bent over the young man's back again, letting out a low moan, and his bare chest closed over the muscular back of the crouched younger man, his taut nipples rubbing against Monte's shoulder blades. He rocked their two torsos ever so slightly, chafing his nipples even more on Monte's back.

Ervin reached around with one hand and cupped Monte's chin and turned and raised Monte's face to him. Monte's lips opened to Ervin's. A growl deep inside Ervin's chest marked the feeble attempt he was making to deny his sin. His free hand went to palm one of Monte's pecs, his thumb finding and rubbing over the nub of Monte's nipple.

The young man's body trembled under the caressing touch of the rough toil-callused hands of the older, more experienced man. Leaving Monte's breast, Ervin's hand moved down Monte's hard belly, unbuttoned the fly of his worn jeans, and wrapped itself around Monte's engorging cock.

Disengaging from the kiss, but their eyes still locked on each other's, Monte gave Ervin a shy look, and asked, almost in a whisper. "You gonna fuck me again today before chores are done, Mr. Walker?"

"Come into the house now," Ervin answered in a hoarse, strangled voice. "The fence is secured good enough for now."

"You gonna fuck me good?"

"Just come into the house, Monte."

"Yes, sir." Obediently, without hesitation, Monte stood and followed Ervin into the house.

Ervin fucked Monte on Monte's bed. It was always on Monte's bed, not Ervin's. Ervin slept in the same bed his parents had slept in—and his father's parent's before that. It was the bed Ervin's mother had birthed him in and the bed both she and his father had died in—the bed Ervin assumed he would die in too. And maybe his son, Tyrone, after him, the son that Ervin's wife had taken away with her when Ervin was discovered to be having his way with Lamont Jackson a couple of farms over.

They fucked on Monte's bed. And they fucked the way Ervin liked it, Monte on all fours or on his belly, and Ervin crouched over his young, well-muscled back, kissing and biting the curves and contours of the young man's back and rubbing his nipples on Monte's shoulder blades, while he stroked Monte's ass in long, deep strokes. Monte panted under Ervin as the older man moved from loving caresses and holding his thick cock at the root and revolving it in Monte's channel, guided by Monte's gasps and murmurs of "yes, there, like that. Fuck me good, Mr. Walker," as Ervin snaked a hand around Monte's waist and stroked his cock to ejaculation.

Monte sexually relieved, Ervin continued stroking, progressively sinking into lust and beyond-control need.

They ended with Monte, always all-out passionate and vocal, not holding out on wanting the fuck, crying out "Ram me! Ram it hard. Yes. Again and again!" And, lost in the primordial fuck, Ervin did just that, pulling out of the younger man's canal with a cry at the end and barely getting the condom ripped off his shaft before he shot his load, in three strong bursts, across the small of Monte's back and collapsed on top of the young man's trembling body.

"That were a good fuck, Mr. Walker. Thank you kindly."

Ervin turned his head, not wanting Monte to see his pained expression, his humiliation of giving into his lust again—and being thanked for it.

Once Monte was into a fuck, he went as whole hog as any young, randy stud, wanting more of it, harder and deeper. And he could be a screamer for it. As casual as he was in giving it away, he could really turn a man on with how intense he was in the clutch.

Sometimes when Ervin felt he wanted the fuck more than once, he'd remain in Monte's bed and they would doze between takings. As submissive as he'd been to the coach's demands in the backseat of his car and grateful to Ervin for taking him in and permitting him to work on the farm for pay before his first year in community college—and feeling protected by having an older man who wanted to make love to his body—Monte uncomplainingly fell in with whatever mood or servicing request Ervin made. He never was the one to ask for a fuck, but he never denied Ervin when Ervin wanted it. He had never denied or hesitated with the coach, either, not even that first time. On occasion, Ervin worried about Monte's pliability, but his own sin was so great that he didn't want to worry about it too much or for too long.

Monte never questioned Ervin's need to gain sexual satisfaction through him at all. The young man's greatest interest was in working on the farm and, specifically, with the animals. Watching animals breed—and sometimes the males trying to breed with each other—was taken by Monte as just the natural way of nature. He assumed that he would ask for sex from Ervin just in the natural scheme of nature if Ervin didn't ask it of him nearly twice a day, fully satiating the needs of even a young, vigorous man in his prime. And Ervin was thicker, could reach deeper, and could stroke longer than Coach Docrity had been able to do. Monte did wonder on occasion whether a younger man could do him even better, but he was in no particular hurry to find out.

He also wondered about being fucked by a white man—if that would be any different from being fucked by the coach or Ervin. He never thought about the morality of being fucked by any man—only about the pleasure he could get and receive from it.

During the day, Ervin could approach and fuck Monte almost anywhere where there was cover. He didn't like to do it out in the open, saying that he couldn't do it with the thought that his sin could be so openly observed from the heavens. But the cover of the shed they called a barn, or inside the pickup cab, or under bushes in the shadow of the house had all been taken advantage of when Ervin's lust got the best of him, which usually was when he saw Monte crouched over, showing the curve of his magnificent, young, hard, bare back.

At night, they always did it in Monte's bed, though. And when he was done, Ervin would return to his own bed, always alone. While moving between the beds, he would admonish himself for giving into his sin. But once in his parents' bed he gave not a whisper of his weakness. In his parents' bed, although a sinner he was, there was no inkling of his deepest, darkest sin. As long as he didn't do it in that bed, surely his ancestors knew nothing of his great failing.

* * * *

"I thought this was all goin' on cross county at the Coles Hill farm."

"EnergyFuture Incorporated is actually looking in several locations." The man answering that was handsome, with the squared-away Marine look, blond buzz cut, and jeans and sport shirt tailored to fit in but still a bit too stylish for Danville.

The question had come from the audience in the library meeting room on the north side of Danville, Virginia. It was the first of the evening that had even a hint of critical question behind it, and Ervin was beginning to be convinced that the movie-star-handsome corporate representative booked to talk to this open meeting on Saturday evening had salted the audience with supporters of the plan to open up a uranium mine in his valley. Thus far the man, who was all smiles and glib talk and flirty looks at the grinning women present, had called on questioners by raised hands. This was resulting in softball questions from folks Ervin had never seen before in his recollection. And Ervin was pretty sure he knew everyone living in the White Creek valley. This last question had been impatiently called out from the audience by one of the valley farmer's Ervin did know, Bill Kemp.

"What about the health hazards of uranium mining?" a woman's thin, crackly voice with a patrician Southern accent floated out over the audience. Ervin could hear a groan go up from many of those in the room he didn't recognize.

"We have plenty of literature on that laid out on the table here, Ms. Harrison. You are welcome to take any of it home with you. And you'll notice that Pittsylvania County's congressional delegation up in Washington has, to a man, written endorsements on those studies."

"Well, Bob, Mark, and Tim are all up in Washington, D.C.," Sadie Harrison called out in a dry voice. "I'm just a bit more interested in the health of those who will be living down here with all that radioactive uranium being brought up from our earth here abouts and refined right here. You did say it was to be refined right here, didn't you?"

The groan, reminiscent of the canned laughter tracts used in TV situation comedies from the previous century, rose again across the audience packed into the windowless library meeting room.

They have come prepared, Ervin thought. That man—Jack Carson, the representative EnergyFuture sent down from Richmond to charm folks into numb brains, to contain and nullify any opposition, and to get land purchases started had done his homework. He even had known who Sadie Harrison was and that she would be a major focus of his problem mitigating the opposition to what EnergyFuture—and Richmond—wanted to do here. She was perhaps the wealthiest person in the northwest corner of the Pittsylvania County. She was as old as the White Oak mountains and her family had been wealthy landowners here since the Revolutionary War. She herself had indexed that she knew everyone who was worth knowing when she had used the first names of the state congressional delegation representing this region in Washington. She also was known as a leading environmental and animal rights advocate in a county known for its ultraconservatism and as a hunter's paradise. She was the major supporter of the county's SPCA, which she insisted maintain a no-kill policy.

As, smiling an "I'm not the least bit worried how this is turning smile," Jack Carson raised his arms to show that he wanted to tamper down the audience reaction before he gave a "reasonable" answer to Sadie Harrison's "obviously" impertinent questions.

Ervin stole a glance at Monte in the folding chair beside his to see what his reaction to all of this was. Monte seemed to be wide-eyed and fascinated. His attention was glued to the handsome, confident-acting man standing on the platform at the front of the room.

"As I noted earlier, the refining aspect is very important for the local economy," Carson said, casting an indulgent smile in the general direction in which Sadie Harrison was sitting in the dimly lit room. "Your political representatives have lobbied hard with EnergyFuture to establish a mine in the White Creek valley area. It will bring several hundred jobs to this region."

"Jobs for folks in Pittsylvania County, or workers from elsewhere?" Lamont Jackson, one of the small-holding farmers a few holdings north of Ervin's farm and Ervin's erstwhile lover called out. Ervin knew that Lamont was one of the farmers who was really hurting and probably would sell out to EnergyFuture if he could—and would probably be one of the first in line for a job with the company if it came here. Although this saddened Ervin, he could understand the financial spot Lamont was in. Lamont's wife hadn't been as forgiving as Ervin's wife had been. She took him for all he was worth, which wasn't much, when she left him.

Of course, it was Ervin's own sin that had led to Lamont's wife leaving him, just as Ervin's wife had left Ervin. That had been enough of a shock—especially having lost visiting rights with his own son—to Ervin that he had been able to deny himself for over a year, during which he lived a solitary life. And then Monte had come to the farm. Monte had not seduced him; he had merely done what Monte did—moved around shirtless, exposing his magnificent back to Ervin. And then, when Ervin's weakness got the better of him, merely lifting his tail to Ervin, as Ervin covered his back, and letting Ervin slide inside him.

"Both, of course," Carson answered. "We would hire in the county and bring in specialists from elsewhere if we could not fill those jobs with local hires. No matter where the workers come from, though, they would be bolstering the region's economy."

Lamont tried a follow-up question on just how many of the jobs would be open to locals and how specialized these jobs were, but Carson was already concentrating on locating the next questioner, and those sitting around Lamont shushed him down.

Carson managed to recognize the raised hand of one of the softball question pitchers, who droned off into a longwinded question that most likely was designed to put everyone to sleep. Instead of dozing, though, Ervin looked over at the large map chart that was an on easel on the platform beside where the company huckster—as Ervin thought of Carson—was positioned.

Ervin had come thinking he'd have to fight for his land, but seeing from the chart on the easel that this wasn't so had kept him more quiet on the question end than he thought he'd be. The chart showed that the boundary of the holdings the company was seeking to acquire came up to the edge of his farm but didn't encroach on it. From the pattern, he could see why this maybe was so. His farm lined up with the vast land holdings of Sadie Harrison—it was Sadie's family that had owned Ervin's once and the small section at the edge of Harrison land that the Walker family had been given. The lines appeared to have been purposely drawn to keep her property out of the holdings the mining company sought, evidently to try to keep her from fighting the acquisition. But if they thought that would satisfy or deter Sadie Harrison, Ervin thought, neither EnergyFuture nor the politicians and lobbyists supporting them in Richmond and Washington knew Sadie Harrison very well. Better that they had waited for the old woman to die. Of course she'd probably outlive everyone in the valley.

Of even greater interest to Ervin in viewing the chart after he had recovered from the discovery that his own land wasn't in danger was the pattern of land already owned by the mining company and that yet to be acquired. The two categories were denoted by different-colored overlays. Viewing the chart revealed that it looked like a crazy quilt. It occurred to Ervin that the company would have to control most of the land and still had to acquire several key acreages owned by others to be able to have a mining operation at all.

He was snapped out of this reverie by another called out question from Bill Kemp, shouted out over the convoluted dissertation being given by the man Carson had recognized from the audience.

"What kind of mine is this going to be? Tunnel or open pit?"

"And what about the radiation problems of an open pit uranium mine?" Sadie Harrison called out. "Won't rain bring up the radiation? And the weather too—we've had hurricanes and tornadoes go through here. Even had an earthquake as recent as three years ago."

"The dangers are minimal at best. Everything is covered in these studies here," Jack Carson answered over the hubbub of those protesting one side of the issue or the other. "But I see someone from the library staff signaling from in back. I'm afraid we'll have to give up the room now. We will, of course, schedule more town meetings on this. We have appreciated the opportunity to tell you what a godsend this will be for this part of Pittsylvania County."

Several residents of the land affected tried to move forward to talk with Carson as the meeting was breaking up, but some of the others were there before them—some of the obvious company plants—and evidently were going to engage in filibuster conversation until there was no time for anyone else to talk with him.

"Let's go, Monte," Ervin said, turning to the young man sitting beside him. "It's obvious this is a put-up job. Should've known. Makes me thirsty. Let's finish the day at the Roadhouse."

At hearing the name of the Roadhouse mentioned Monte came out of the trance he was in of watching the hunky-looking representative of EnergyFuture Incorporated continue to work the room. They'd serve him anything he wanted there, and it was a bar, out in the country off of

Route 29 between Danville and Chatham, where the likes of Ervin and he could be comfortable.

Giving Ervin a big smile, he uncoiled from the folding chair and voiced a cheery, "Ready." Still, his gaze remained on the squared-away Marine type, Jack Carson, until he and Ervin had cleared the meeting room.

As they got into the truck, Ervin said, trying to make it sound off hand, "You looked at that white man like you could eat him. He's city and white, Monte. Not in the same universe with you."

"Ain't seen a white man put together that good is all," Monte answered. "Still, I wouldn't say no if he wanted to eat me."

It was all said so naturally. Ervin gripped the steering wheel hard. Ervin wondered if Monte would ever lose his innocence about sex. He hoped not.

* * * *

Ervin didn't give a second thought as to anyone else, certainly not anyone he didn't want to see, going on from the uranium mine proposal meeting to the Roadhouse bar, which was a good twenty miles north of Danville. The Roadhouse catered to men like Ervin—and now Monte—in the evening hours, men who enjoyed the company of men and who might leave the place with a man they didn't come in with. Later, after midnight, it was likely to get rowdy and there'd be some entertainment on the platform by the bar, most likely put on by the young black guy, Slick, who took care of the table trade earlier in the evening. There might even be some action in one or more of the back rooms down the corridor to the john.

The meeting had gone on longer than Ervin thought it would, so he and Monte were arriving at the bar near to 11:30, within the transition time for clientele. All Ervin intended to do was to have one drink there and go on home and, because he was so keyed up from the meeting, fuck Monte silly. He'd make Monte forget the white man at the meeting. He didn't want to stay until midnight mainly because he didn't like having Monte in the bar for the late-night crowd. Monte was like honey to the latter-shift men, who tended to be rough trade, truck drivers and construction workers from down in Danville. Ervin didn't want Monte getting sniffed around by men like this. Monte was of a pretty basic nature, and it was clear that he felt no guilt about having sex with men. Ervin was afraid that the late-night clientele would eat Monte up—and that Monte just might let them.

As willing as Monte was, Ervin was confident that there had only been the coach and him. Monte had no concept of what a gang bang by truckers could be.

Ervin was only half way through his drink, though, when he was given reason to stay on past midnight. Speaking of the devil, which Ervin had occasion to talk about from time to time, he was about to chug his drink and tell Monte to down his too so they could leave, Ervin not liking the look being cast Monte's way from a burly guy with big muscles and curly red hair who had been getting out of a semitrailer out front when Ervin and Monte drove up, when who walked through the door but Lamont Jackson. And behind him, already looking like he owned the place, came that EnergyFuture shyster, Jack Carson.

As soon as Carson saw Monte, he gave a big smile, which then turned, but only briefly, to more of a scowl when he saw Ervin standing alongside Monte at the bar. Ervin could see, out of the corner of his eye, that Monte was returning the smile.

Slick almost ran to Lamont and Carson to show them to a table and to pay particular attention to Carson. Ervin had to allow that Carson wasn't the hulkiest guy in the bar now, but he probably was the hunkiest one. In the phenomena that exists in instant selection in male-on-male cruising, most of the catchers in the room were casting eyes of interest on Carson, while most of the pitchers—who until now had been watching Monte—were eyeing him as possible competition. Slick was nearly drooling over him and couldn't get him anything he wanted fast enough.

Ervin knew that Lamont was one of the guys—it had been Ervin himself who had initiated Lamont to this life— but he was surprised that Carson was. Since the man was in this environment, though, there was no doubting by the way he cased the room, that he knew what kind of bar this was and why he was here—and that he could get any bottom in the room to lie down for him and open his legs to him.

But his eyes kept going to Monte.

Lamont didn't seem too happy to be here with him, but no doubt Carson had correctly gauged Lamont's leaning either at the meeting or earlier in land purchase discussions with him, and had pressed Lamont to bring him here. He'd had time to lay Lamont between the meeting and arriving here, and Ervin saw no reason not to assume that he'd done so. It also seemed evident that Carson knew that they would be following Ervin and Monte here—and that Carson's primary interest was in Monte. Something in the disappointment Lamont showed told Ervin that, no matter what Carson had done with Lamont, the interest he'd shown in talking with Lamont was in Monte—that even as he was pumping Lamont's ass, he probably was asking him about Monte.

Ervin hadn't been aware of the buildup to this back at the meeting, but now, in hindsight, having Carson's interests pegged, he realized that Carson had been doing a whole lot of looking in Monte's direction. He already knew that Monte had done lots of looking at Carson, and Monte had been straight-up open afterward about his interest in Carson.

Ervin turned his face toward the bar and ordered another beer and told Monte he could have one too. Then he put a possessive arm around Monte and Monte just sort of folded into him. Ervin didn't need the drink, but he wanted to invest a little time into signaling to Carson that Monte was taken. That's why they'd be staying longer in the bar than he originally had intended to.

He took a couple of peeks in the direction of the table that Lamont and Carson were sitting at and saw that they were deep in conversation—probably haggling over the sale of Lamont's farm—and that Slick was still buzzing around them. The next thing he knew, though, when he took a look, Carson was no longer at the table, and Lamont was sinking into his glass of beer and looking not the least bit happy.

Ervin looked around the room but didn't see the huckster from Richmond. He half expected to find that he was circling in on Monte even though Ervin still had the young man in a clutch, but he just wasn't around.

"Stay put here for a few minutes, and drink up," Ervin said to Monte. "I have to go take a piss, and we'll go on home when I get back."

"Sure thing," Monte said. There were some wooden puzzles scattered out on the bar top, and Monte was absorbed in trying to put one of those together.

The john was at the end of a corridor off the back through a doorway covered with a beaded curtain. There were small rooms off the corridor on either side on the way back that were rented out in fifteen-minute increments. Ervin saw, in passing to the back, that Jack Carson and Slick occupied one of these rooms. Carson was seated on the side of a cot and Slick was kneeling between his thighs and sucking him off. When Ervin returned from the john, Carson had proceeded to pull Slick onto his lap, both of them naked from the waist down, and was lap fucking the young man. Slick was revolving his ass on Carson's buried dick and his tongue was lolling out of his mouth like he'd never been fucked this good before, which was hard to believe as often as he'd been spiked.

Good, Ervin thought. That will hold the fucker long enough for me to get Monte out of the bar.

But Ervin had a different problem when he pushed through the beaded curtain and out into the main room. Monte appeared to be gone already. His beer glass was empty and the puzzle he'd been working on was put together—Monte was clever in fixing things—but Monte wasn't in the room. Neither was the muscle-bound, red-headed trucker.

He found them out in the parking lot. The passenger-side door—the one toward the shadows at the back of the parking lot—of the semitrailer's cab was hanging open. The trucker, bare legged, was standing on the running board, facing the interior of the cab. Monte's construction booted-feet were wedged at the top of the door frame, front and back. His legs were bare otherwise as well. From the movement of the trucker and the grunts and groans, Ervin knew that Monte was getting fucked hard and fast.

He didn't intervene. The trucker was a lot bigger, more heavily muscled, and very likely much meaner than Ervin was. The trucker also was white and there was a filled gun rack mounted on the back wall of the semi cab, which Ervin clearly could see, and which the trucker could get to before Ervin could get anywhere close to him. The trucker also could come back to finish up any business he felt he needed to finish up. Ervin hadn't survived in this rural part of Virginia by taking risks and asserting rights. And he had no right to Monte, really. If the young man wanted a younger man than Ervin fucking him from time to time, Ervin didn't really see that he could kick about that.

And from the noises Monte was making, he was clearly enjoying himself. Ervin just wished that Monte didn't give it away so easily and naturally. Even there, though, Ervin, who was very much aware of his own sinning in this respect, wasn't going to be hypocritical about how easily Monte was prepared to give it away.

116

After the trucker was finished, he pretty much pulled Monte out of the cab and deposited him on the ground in a heap. He then pulled on his jeans and was zipping himself up as he walked around the front of the truck, got in the driver's side, and pulled the semi out of the parking lot and down the road, not even glancing back at Monte.

Ervin rushed over to Monte's side, but he could clearly see that Monte was moaning and had a big grin on his face. He was still humming and giving a little smile in the Ford pickup on the way back to White Creek valley. All that he said was, "He gave me twenty dollars, and he had a right good cock. First white man I've had."

When Ervin got him back in the farmhouse and on his bed, Monte allowed as how Ervin had a right good cock too—and that from what he'd experienced so far, black cock was a whole lot bigger than white cock.

Ervin didn't fuck him in anger. It was more with relief that Monte didn't show any change in opening up for Ervin after having it rough from a trucker and in a concern at how innocent Monte seemed to be and how easily he could be taken advantage of—and some anger at himself for not being able to resist joining those who couldn't resist fucking Monte.

A large part of the attraction to Ervin of Monte was the young man's earthiness—how naturally he took to the sex, how willing he was to celebrate it and to give and take without constraint—and how gloriously beautiful he was in his natural state. Ervin felt the same way about Monte that he felt about his own farm and about White Oak valley.

* * * *

Chock full of remorse but fully recognizing that the flesh wasn't going to lose its weakness anytime soon, on Sunday morning, in the old one-room schoolhouse in Pleasant Gap that his mother had converted into a church,

Ervin gave an impassioned sermon on the word he'd been given on the ridgetop the previous Friday—sacrifice. He was just letting the word pour through and out of him as it would. He had little idea what he was preaching, and the five other people in the small room—the Lincoln sisters on the front row, whispering gossip to each other; old Jethro, dozing and his hearing aide turned off three rows back; and the spooning couple right on the back row—weren't trying very hard to follow him either.

In the middle of his gyrations, Ervin stopped dead in his tracks. For the first time he really paid attention to the word—to the word "sacrifice." None of the others seemed to realize he'd even stopped. The meaning of the word suddenly hit him—not the meaning for this sermon, but the meaning for what was going on in the life of the valley.

Pronouncing a quick benediction, with the Lincoln sisters suddenly becoming aware, in shock and guilty pleasure, that the service was drawing to a close—a full half hour earlier than usual—Ervin bowed to the faithful and nearly ran from the building, headed back to the farm to begin a series of phone calls, calling a meeting for that evening.

* * * *

Ervin and Monte were belly up to the bar at the Roadhouse in the hour approaching midnight on Monday night. Ervin had never brought Monte here before on a Monday night, and it didn't escape Monte that this was unusual. For the first time the young man seemed to be nervous being here. To a great extent the crowd there was composed of the same men who had been there Saturday night. That wasn't particularly a surprise, because Pittsylvania County was a sparsely populated rural one, and there are only so many men around such an area who were out in the open enough to come to the Roadhouse regularly. Lamont Jackson

118

was there, as was Slick. Slick seemed always to be there. The trucker from Saturday night wasn't there, but Ervin figured he wouldn't be there—hoped he wouldn't be there; counted on him not being there, in view of how often Monte had mentioned how much he'd enjoyed being rough fucked half in and half out of the semi cab—because he wasn't a regular patron of the Roadhouse. Ervin figured he'd just been passing through on a long-haul transport.

Lamont was standing with Ervin and Monte at the bar. Monte was fidgeting, looking around the room, once again a major attraction, but not being able to hold eye contact with any of the men who obviously wanted him.

Along about 11:30, even Jack Carson was there, having come in, looked around, spied Monte and smiled, and then gone to a table to be slobbered over by Slick. Monte settled down a bit after Carson appeared and did give him shy smiles now and again. But the hand that picked up his beer glass still trembled like it never had before in the Roadhouse.

Not more than fifteen minutes after that, the fire sirens started going off, following the telephone lines up from Chatham. There was such a siren on the roof of the Roadhouse, but the signal was heard from up Route 29 before it got to the Roadhouse. Ervin and a couple of the other men were chugging their beers at the first sound of the distant alarm and preparing to race their trucks to the nearest fire house, which was in the small town of Dry Fork. Ervin was a volunteer fireman; Monte wasn't.

"I gotta answer the call," Ervin told Monte in a loud voice. "You need to catch a ride back to the farm with someone else. Lamont can take you." Ervin didn't wait for an answer. He pushed off from the bar and headed out to his truck.

Ervin had said that loud enough for the whole room to have heard him, it would seem, so he had every reason to assume that Lamont had. But the siren had just gone off on the roof, so there was competition for his voice.

Whether or not Lamont heard Ervin, about ten minutes after Ervin left, so did Lamont—without taking Monte. Monte had been looking over at the table where Jack Carson sat—looking back at Monte—and he didn't even notice Lamont leaving. He looked around and, not seeing Lamont anywhere, he looked back at Jack Carson's table. Jack Carson was smiling and waving for Monte to join him. Monte took a deep swig of his beer, breathed deeply, almost hiccupping from the nervous catch in his breath, and pushed off from the bar.

Half way back to Ervin's farm from the Roadhouse, Jack Carson pulled his EnergyFuture Land Rover off onto a lane leading to the banks of White Oak Creek. He cut off the engine and turned in the seat, facing Monte.

"You know I've had my eye on you since the meeting down in Danville," he said in a low, hoarse voice. "You're a right fine strapping young man."

"I 'spose," Monte said shyly, his legs spread and his arms hanging down between them. He was looking down at the floor mat between his legs.

"You haven't asked why I pulled off the road."

Monte didn't answer or look up.

"You're not the least bit curious why?"

"I reckon I know why."

"And it doesn't bother you?"

"I reckon not."

"You know what kind of bar that was that we were just in, don't you, Diamonte?" It didn't escape Monte that Carson had taken the time to learn his name. Monte hadn't given him a name.

"They call me Monte. Yes, I know."

"That man I always see you with, the scratch farmer, Ervin Walker. Is he your man? Do you lie under him?"

"Yeah, he's my man. He fucks me."

120

"I heard tell you got fucked out in the parking lot Saturday night by a trucker. That true?"

"Yeah. It was OK. He paid me. He had a good cock."

"And this Walker guy. Did he know about it? Was it OK with him?"

"Seems like. He lets me make my own decisions, do what I want."

"Lift your head and look at me, Monte."

Monte did so, but he didn't only look into Carson's eyes. Carson's thick cock was rising up outside of his fly and standing straight up.

"You see how I'm interested in you, how badly I want you, Monte? Do you like the looks of me as well as that trucker? Or Walker? You going to make me work hard at this?"

There was a pause, and then, letting his held breath out in a long sigh, Monte said, "No, sir."

"No what?"

"No, I ain't gonna make you work hard for it. I knew this was what you wanted when you pulled off the road. I knew it when you offered me the ride home. I knew it was what you wanted when you invited me over to the table."

"I'll pay you fifty dollars for it."

"That would be right nice, thank you."

Carson leaned over and, putting his hands on either side of Monte, brought his face in for a kiss. The kiss didn't last too long, though. Carson obviously was anxious to get right to business. Without releasing Monte's face, coming out of the kiss, Carson just continued pulling Monte's face down to his lap onto his already-released, engorging cock.

"Suck it for me, please, Monte, and then I'm going to fuck you."

They fucked in the backseat of the Land Rover, with Monte giving Carson his money's worth by straddling the thighs of the sitting older man, facing him, and riding Carson's thick cock.

Carson encircled Monte's body with his arms and nuzzled his face into Monte's shoulder as they cooled off from the fuck in which they had ejaculated nearly simultaneously, Carson filling up the bulb of a Magnum and Monte shooting off up Carson's flat belly. His pent up lust taken care of, Carson wanted to take more time playing. His lips went to Monte's nipples and Monte arched his back to accommodate Carson's play. They kissed now in long, breathtaking moments with plenty of tonguing.

"That was extra nice," Carson said as they came out of a kiss.

"You're extra big," Monte murmured.

"You cramping? You want to come off it?"

"No, not yet. I like you deep inside me. We can do it again, if you want. You don't have to pay more. I liked it. Your cock is as good as a black man's."

"God, you seem so natural and casual with it. Are you this way with any man who wants to fuck you?"

"Not just anyone. But the ones I want to fuck, yes."

"It's a turn-on that you take it natural like this."

"Why not? Animals fuck. We're animals, ain't we? It's the way of nature. If you want me and I want you, why not?"

"Why not indeed? And tomorrow you can let Ervin Walker fuck you too and you feel no guilt that I fucked you tonight?"

"No. Why? Mr. Walker, he don't own me. And he says he sees it that way too. Otherwise I'd probably not be with him. And it's only for the summer."

"Only for the summer? So you aren't tied to Walker?"

"No, I'm goin' to community college in the fall."

"I see. I'd like to see you again. You think Walker would let you be out for a night?"

"Uh, I'm not sure . . ."

"I'd pay you a hundred dollars for a night."

"Well, then . . ."

122

"I've got use of a cabin over on the Dan River below Boyd's mountain. Maybe in a week or two . . ."

"Why not right now?"

"Now's not a good time. I've got these land deals to work. Another couple of weeks and . . . oh shit . . . what the fuck!"

Monte had swiveled around on the cock, facing the front of the Land Rover. He had planted the heels of his feet in the floor of the vehicle and gripped the tops of the front seats with his hands and was pushing back and forth with his channel on Carson's cock, fucking himself hard and deep on the shaft. Immediately lost to the moment, Carson grabbed Monte's waist in his hands and helped with the push and pull as he threw his head back and howled to the ceiling of the vehicle.

"Cabin now. Cabin now," Monte was chanting in a mantra.

They were barely in the front door of the cabin, when Carson pushed Monte down on all fours on an oval braided rug, mounted him like a dog, and rode him for a half hour.

On the second day, when Carson's interest seemed to be flagging a bit, Monte begged to be fucked in the shower and then to have his wrists bound to the headboard and for Carson to punish him roughly. Any time there was a gleam in Carson's eyes in response to something that could be done in sex, Monte wanted to do it. There was nothing that Carson could conceivably think of asking Monte to do that Monte wouldn't do.

Monte kept Carson in the Dan River cabin for three days, riding the cock and being ridden by the cock in every conceivable location and position and time of day or night.

On the afternoon of the third day, Carson asked Monte to go back with him to Richmond. There he could enroll in a community college that Carson would pay for, and Carson would set him up in a small apartment. Carson's wife need know nothing of the arrangement, Carson said. He had gotten away with such an arrangement before.

* * * *

The afternoon of the fourth day Ervin had the hood up on his Ford pickup and was seeing what he could do about keeping the truck going through another winter, when he sensed he wasn't alone. He looked up and saw Monte opening the gate of the fence surrounding the farm yard. The young man looked hot and tired—as if he'd been walking for miles. And, as it turned out, he had been. Jack Carson had let him off out on Route 41, and Monte had walked the dusty dirt back road into the farm.

As Monte approached, Ervin came out from underneath the hood and turned toward the young man. Monte was only wearing jeans and was barefoot. Ervin was the same.

"You've come back."

"Yes."

"To pick up your things or to stay?"

"To stay through the summer. Like we agreed."

"You been with that EnergyFuture huckster, Jack Carson, all this time?"

"Yes, sir."

"Thought so. Haven't seen him around."

"Was it long enough?"

"Yes."

"Good."

"He treat you right?"

"Nothing to complain about."

"OK, then. Best you get under the spigot and wash down."

Ervin watched Monte as the young man went over to the spigot next to the horse trough. He unbuttoned his fly

124

and stripped off his jeans. Then he bent over to get his head under the spigot.

A low growl came up from deep inside Ervin's chest and, trembling, he walked to Monte, stripping off his own jeans as he moved. His eyes were on the curve of Monte's naked back. That image was what aroused Ervin the most. And it had been four days of foregoing his needs, living the sacrifice.

Monte felt the strong hands on his waist, and he moved to the side, as they guided him, coming down on his belly on the rim of the nearly empty horse trough, letting his head drop down into the trough and grabbing the far rim of the trough with his fists, while Ervin kissed and stroked his back with gliding hands. There was no resistance in the young man whatsoever. It was like he hadn't been gone the three days and more. There'd be no apologizing—indeed Ervin couldn't imagine that there would be—and Monte was as ready to be spiked by Ervin as he ever was.

Ervin's hands glided down Monte's back from his shoulder blades to the small of his back, where they fanned outward to the young man's hips. Monte raised his hips as Ervin's meaty cockhead moved into the crack and dragged across the puckering hole, again and again, while Monte gasped and sighed.

"Yes," Monte murmured in a husky voice, "Put it in me. Fuck me, Daddy. Be good to me."

There was no hesitancy, no resistance.

Ervin's hands tightened over Monte's bulbous buttocks and spread them as his cock head pressed against the hole and pressed into the cavity.

Monte gasped and pushed back on the cock, taking it inside him. "Ride me, Daddy. Fuck me deep."

So natural; so giving, Ervin thought. No hesitancy in the young man. Freely giving and taking pleasure. So . . . earthy. It would be a sacrifice to give him up.

Then Ervin was inside Monte, stroking him vigorously and hard and singing his hallelujahs to the noonday sun above, not caring who or what saw them. Though this be sin, his mind screamed, he would make the most of it.

Thrusting again and again. Monte pushing his rump back onto the cock, crying for more of it, deeper and harder. The two of them coming in a gush, almost simultaneously, Ervin flooding Monte's channel deep, as the urgency had provided no opportunity for niceties. Monte arching back to him after the ejaculation, the two men kissing deeply, Monte whispering that Ervin could do it again, if he wanted. Monte not begging for it now, but not avoiding it either. Always ready, always open for it.

After lunch, they both climbed up the White Oak mountain ridge, sat near to each other on a rock, and stared down into the valley. It was Friday, Ervin's day to open himself to the word for Sunday's preaching. He was too full of the moment, though, to meditate. He wanted Monte up here for a time—to see and understand what he had sacrificed for. Afterward, Ervin would send him back down to the farm and would mediate for a word. He would cheat today, though. He sometimes did, but he always pretended that the word only came to him after meditating up here. He already knew, however, that the word that would come to him today would be "thanksgiving."

"See how beautiful it is down there?" Ervin asked.

"Yes."

"Pristine farm land. Never developed as anything else but fields and meadows—for more than three hundred years—and maybe longer, by the Indians, before that."

They were both silent for a few minutes, their hands entwined.

"And, thanks to you, it will stay that way."

They were silent again, gazing out over the valley.

126

"Did you have any trouble getting that Carson guy to drive you away after I left on the false fire alarm I set up and Lamont left as planned too?"

"No, none at all. You managed with the land sales OK?" Monte asked.

"Yes, Sadie Harrison hauled out her checkbook. The three days that EnergyFuture shyster could have been making land deals but was holed up with you somewhere, Sadie was buying up from whoever wanted to sell. Lamont Jackson's already sold out and gone from the valley. There's no way that EnergyFuture bastard's going to get that land from Sadie. She's already arranging to put it in the nature conservancy, so not even death is going to help them."

"So, we got what we wanted?"

"Yep. EnergyFuture can't get enough parcels of land together now to put in the uranium mine here. Sadie rattled the government in Richmond and came up with information not contained in any of those pamphlets they gave us. Only an open-pit strip mine would work here, it seems. All that radiation exposed and going up in the air morning, noon, and night, and probably coming back down as far away as Danville and Chatham. Now if they want to do their mining here in Virginia, they'll have to go back across the county to that Coles Farm tract. And that can be an underground mine. Still dangerous, but not like they wanted to do here."

"I'm glad you got what you wanted and the valley will stay as it is," Monte said.

"I hope it wasn't too much of a sacrifice, son," Ervin said. "I didn't know of any other way to get those three days out ahead of the Carson snake. I knew it had to be by sacrifice. I hope that brute wasn't too rough on you. I hated asking you to do that for us—keeping him occupied to give Sadie time to buy the land out from underneath him. But what we did here, we did for the glory of the earth. Can't do no better than honor the earth, my momma always said."

"Naw, it was OK," Monte said. He turned away from Ervin, so that the older man couldn't see him smile. "One thing I thought of while I was gone, though," Monte said.

"What's that?"

"I think rather than going into Danville for community college in the fall, I'll go up to Richmond. I think prospects there might be better than down here."

"Whatever suits you, son."

"You would be OK with that?"

"It will be a sad day when you move on, of course. But you have been a sin that I must work on. Not your doing, of course, other than being here. My weakness. You've made such a sacrifice for this valley. It will be my turn to make a sacrifice too. Not today or tomorrow, of course. But, yes, going to Richmond will be a good idea; you should find friends of your own age there. And I've ever said I have no hold over you, that you can do what you like."

"I think I'd like that . . . going to Richmond. I got a friend there who says he'll put me up while I'm going to college."

Monte had to stay turned so that Ervin couldn't see how hard he was smiling about just how much he thought he was going to like that. As sacrifices go, it had been a pretty easy one—a lot more enjoyable than he'd thought it would be. That Jack had a cock as good as a black man's.

~

About the Author

Habu is one of the pen names of a former supersonic spy jet pilot, intelligence agent, male model, movie actor, and diplomat. A wild youth in South East Asia was spent enjoying whatever sexual opportunities came his way, and much of his gay male writing is about recalling incidents from those days and inventing ones he'd perhaps have liked to experience. He now leads a very quiet and ordinary happily married family life.

An American, he is a published mainstream novelist and short story writer under another name and in another dimension of his life. He has written or cowritten (with Sabb) approaching 1,000 published short stories and over 100 published erotica e-books, primarily of gay fiction but also memoir, straight fiction and ménage fiction. His hand and creative writing can be seen in stories and books by habu, sr71plt, Dirk Hessian, Shabbu, and Stephen Kessel—among unrevealed others that might surprise readers. The fictionalized GM memoir *Flying High, Diving Deep* is loosely based on his life experiences. He can be found at the adults only gay male site www.BarbarianSpy.com, which he shares with Sabb and Dirk Hessian.

Our authors always like to receive feedback, and appreciate it when readers post reviews at distributors and other sites.

BarbarianSpy

FOR LITERARY HEAT

Not all books listed below may currently be on release.
* indicates the book is available in paperback and e-book.
BOOKS BY CHRIS CROSS
Multisexual Adult Romance
Pulaski Square
BOOKS BY ALEX LOCKHEED
Transgender Romance
Meeting Jenna
Transgender Other
Being Sarah
BOOKS BY DIRK HESSIAN
Xtreme Historical Erotica
The King's Men
Shores of Tripoli
Prophecy of Noto
Pretender's Fate
General Historical Erotic Romance
To the Hessian Hills
Fire Down the Valley*
Constantinople*
The Beautiful Way*
Blue and Gray
Colonel's Treasure
Beginning of Time
Labyrinth
BOOKS BY HABU
Gay Erotica
Memoir Faction
Flying High, Diving Deep*

Xtreme Erotica
Tramp Steaming*
Escape to Girne
Silas' Choice*
Last Call
Choke Hold
Apyko: The Greek Pimp
Visits of the Schlange
Second Coming: Emile La Cour Unleashed
Vortex: Sacrificed by Curiosity*
Dark Angel Sounding *(in e-book & included in Sounding:Ultimate Control Paperback)*
Sounding: Ultimate Control (*Print Only*)*
Sounding Five *(in e-book & included in Sounding:Ultimate Control paperback)**

Romance
Rain Check
Built for Pleasure (Sci Fi)
Danny's Choice
Pull of the Groove
Sugar n Spice Christmas
Friday Nights with Lenny (Christmas Romance)
Snowy, Snowy Nights (Christmas Romance)
Tank n Bull
Sail to the Sun
War Letters
Ravens Roost
Caribbean Cruise Top to Bottom
Arena Stage
Trading Partners (Valentine's Day)
Four Coins
Lower Than the Heart (Valentine's Day)
Brambleton
Gotta Keep Trying
Finding Amnad
Platres Conclave

Other Novels/Novellas
TemptationsClutches*

Descent into Chaos
Escape to Girne
Journey Through Abilene
Harmony and Dissonance
Stallion Station
Racing With the Devil (espionage suspense)
Cruising Gigolo (bisexual)
Prepared in Cape Verdi
Gilded Cage
House on Park*
Anything for Ambition
Dance of the Ravishers
Hard Knocks U*
My Neighbor's Spa*
Man's Man: Tales of a High Priced Gay Hooker*
Trip Money
The Indian Doctor
Sailorboy
Home to Fire Island
Murder Mysteries
Death on a Ping Pong Table
Clint Folsom Mysteries Compendium Volume 1*
Death to Blonds - Stolen Judgment (Clint Folsom
Mystery)*
Clint Folsom Mysteries Compendium Volume 2*
Gay Erotica Anthologies
Earth Cry*
Shunga
Habu's Christmas Balls
Eight in D*
DevilMENt
Silas' Choices*
Stallion Station (A Novella in Parts)
Eleven to the Dogs*
Fifty Seventy*
Spy Tails 001*
Spy Tails 002*
Doubled*

Doubled Again*
Tails in the Tropics*
Tails in the Med*
Tails in the West*
Rough Riders*
Grab Bag 1*
Grab Bag 2*
Grab Bag 3*
Grab Bag 4*
Grab Bag 5*
Grab Bag 6*
Grab Bag 7*
Beyond the Beaded Curtain*
Habu's Christmas Balls
The Sporting Life*
Fetish Galore!*
Literary Gay Erotica
Cairo Surrender*
The Handyman*
Homeward Bound
Journey to Mirage*
Bi-Sexual/Menage Erotica
Bisexual/Menage/Multisexual Erotica
Two Men, One Woman*
Every Which Way
Vanishing Laura
Summer of Denial
Death on a Ping Pong Table
Cruising Gigolo
13 Ways for Halloween
Luther*
The Indian Prince*
MF Erotica
Chocolate in Vanilla*
BOOKS BY SABB
Driver Reliever
Hiring in Hollywood
The Legend of Holleystone Grange

Surprise Encounters*
She is He
Wrong Man
Loyal to his King
Barbarian Tales - Book One - Traveler's Tales*
Barbarian Tales - Book Two - Journeys Begin*
Barbarian Tales - Book Three - The Inheritance*
Barbarian Tales - Book Four - Road to Persepolis*

BOOKS BY SHABBU
Velvet Interrogation
Finding Jason
Dirty Pool
Operation Black Jade
Cigars!*
Angel in the Barn
Gayly Complicated*
Despoiling David
The Tree of Idleness*
I Met a Man
Rough Road to Happiness

BOOKS BY STEPHEN KESSEL
Gay Romance
The Forever Man
Two Chances

BOOKS BY KIM BLACK
Lesbian Romance
Transfixed on Tammie (F/T lesbian)